PRAISE FOR THE CLEANSING

"Really builds in unsettling intensity. A great read!"
— John Locke, author of *The Thing's Incredible! The Secret Origins of Weird Tales.*

"Reading this book is reminiscent of the best of the old pulps. It is also a very visual experience. It is easy to imagine this book as a movie."
— Jack and Carole Bender, artist-writers of the famed *Alley Oop* comic strip

"Recently finished reading a series of WEIRD TALES stories before devouring this book, and it felt like I never left!"
— Chad Calkin

"*The Cleansing* will bear mentioning in the same breath with Lovecraft and Robert Bloch and Robert E. Howard, with as compelling a voice as any such Architects of the Weird."
— Michael H. Price, *Forgotten Horrors*

SATAN'S SWINE

THE CLEANSING: BOOK 2

ROBERT A. BROWN
JOHN WOOLEY

BABYLON
BOOKS

This one's for John McMahan, a true friend to both of us and a great collector as well.

INTRODUCTION

If you're reading these words, then you have discovered the trove of extraordinary letters written to me by my best friend, Robert A. Brown, beginning in early May, 1939, when he was assigned by the WPA to take down stories told by old people living in the remote hills of Arkansas. Using Ma Stean's government-approved boarding house in the little burg of Mackaville as his base of operations, Robert set out to do his job. But it didn't take him long to realize that something lurked beneath the town's bucolic surface, a bubbling cauldron of eldritch mysteries that even his seventh sense couldn't completely penetrate.

That's right. His seventh sense.

As you'll see from our correspondence, Robert is blessed with a gift of being able to see and feel things before they happen. I assure you this is something real; we've both

known about it since we were grade school
classmates in Hallock, Minn. He doesn't always
know what's coming up, but he does sometimes.
I've seen it happen way too many times to even
suggest that it's the bunk.

What I've seen is not important, though.
It's what he saw. From the very minute he
disembarked at the train station in Mackaviile
and had to fight a couple of the local hill-
billies to get his typewriter back, he encountered one inexplicable situation after another.
There were cats that seemed to be people, and
people who seemed to be cats. There were igno-
rant-sounding moonshiners who turned out to be
the owners of the town's only real industry,
the packing plant, and big-time hog farmers to
boot.

The people themselves were unusual, too, all
mixed up between Negro and white, thanks to the
Scotsman who organized the town long ago and
gave it its name. Coffee-and-cream colored,
Robert called them.

The two dim-wits who tried to steal his
typewriter showed up again in even more
dangerous ways. So did their father, a character named Old Man Black, who seems
constructed of pure evil. Robert swore the old
boy exerted some sort of power over snakes, and
he should know — he bore the brunt of Black's
dark powers.

I don't mean to say Robert's life was unre-
lenting horror. There was the kind owner of the
boarding house and Pete, the man from the gas

station who rented Robert a motorcycle for his travels. And maybe most of all, there was a young lady named Patricia to help make things bearable.

But there was always danger. It's important for people to know that, and to know that Robert did not give up or try to run away. Instead, he stayed and fought back. At one point, he had me send him some of his magic books from home to aid in that fight. He believed they had power in their pages, and I couldn't argue with him — although I'll always wonder if the magic escalated his conflict with the Blacks, the one that finally led to Robert being hospitalized.

Thinking back, I don't exactly know why I wrote this introduction, except maybe to caution the reader about what he's going to find here and also to let him know that because Robert entrusted me with these letters, I kept them stored away in good condition, just as he asked.

You, whoever you might be, have found Robert's incredible story. You'll want to read every word, because there's a lot more to it. A lot more…

Sincerely,

John Wooley

July 7, 1939
  Friday afternoon

Dear John,

First of all, I want to tell you again that your telephone calls made me feel real good. I'll bet they're a big reason I'm now back in my own bed at Ma's instead of still lying around at Dodd General. You helped me keep my spirits up while I was in the valley of the shadow, and I know that you meant it when you told me you'd leave everything and get down here if I needed you.

But you've done enough — more than enough. Long-distance from St. Paul to Harrison, Arkansas ain't cheap, chum, and I hope those calls didn't eat up that fat check you're getting from old Farnsworth Wright at Weird Tales.

Thanks, too, for taking care of my folks. I know Dad wanted to jump in his Terraplane and head south as soon as he heard from Dr. Jennings, but that wouldn't have done any good really. I know you talked him out of it and that was the right thing. I didn't realize until you told me that Dr. Jennings was hanging crepe about my chances of survival and that couldn't have done you or my folks any good. I think he was just preparing you for the worst. I don't blame him, I guess. There for a while I wasn't sure I'd make it back to the land of the living myself.

Anyway, the worst didn't happen and I am now just resting up, a little weak but otherwise feeling pretty jake, all things considered. Like I told you a couple of days ago on the telephone, I hated like hell to be laid up on Independence Day — as you well know, it's a great favorite holiday of mine — but at least they wheeled my bed over in front of the window at dusk so I could see their town's fireworks celebration. A crackerjack display, but not nearly as much fun as we used to have with our Roman candles and mortar shells and experimental homemade explosives.

Don't think I'm complaining. I can't kick about the treatment I got in the hospital. They brought me through. Pete and Diffie and Ma all came up to visit. Even old Doc Chavez drove all the way to Harrison to check on me. And then Patricia — well, I guess Ma let her off from work quite a little bit, because the first thing I saw when I came to was her, and since I'd been out for almost two days, as I found out later, I suspect she'd been sitting in my room for quite a spell.

Focusing my blurry eyes on that sweet face, right by my bedside, was like waking up with an angel. I guess she heard me stir or make a noise, because she jumped up, her Liberty dropping to the floor, and smiled a smile so dazzling that I thought I'd somehow died and made it to the Pearly Gates.

"Robert!" she said, grabbing me by the shoulders. "Thank God!" I tried to reach for her and pull her to me, but I couldn't quite get the message to my body. She said some more things and kissed me on the forehead and before I knew it the room was bustling. The nurse stuck a thermometer in my mouth and Dr. Jennings poked at me and "hmmmmed" at the nurse and lifted up my left arm, which was still pretty sore and puffy. And then they were gone, and it was just Patricia in the room, sitting next to me and holding my hand across the railing of the hospital bed. I fell asleep again, just as easy as floating away to heaven on a cloud.

It still took a few days before the doc pronounced me out of danger. Even then, Patricia still made the drive up every day after helping Ma serve breakfast and stayed until she had to go back for dinnertime at the boarding house. One time, she even brought me a couple of pulps from the twofer rack at Sparky's Market for a surprise. I could tell how proud she was about picking them out herself, and she didn't do too bad: a Terror Tales (I doubt she would've chosen that one if she'd thought to look at any of the stories in it) and a Thrilling Wonder Stories. I had to put the Terror Tales down after reading a couple of novelettes because they were giving me bad dreams, but there was some pretty good space opera, as usual, in the Thrilling Wonder.

A couple of times Mrs. Davis came along with Patricia, and that old lady was very nice to me, maybe because I never tried to get her to talk about any of the weird stuff about the cats and all. Right now, I just don't want to bring any of that up around Patricia — even though I'd thought a lot about it and the snakes and pigs and everything else while I was lying there in the hospital. Remember that old military acronym OBE — Overtaken by Events? I think that's what happened to me. The attack in the mountains, the fight with the Blacks, the snake in my room, the Gabbers and the pig and rattler war, and then this hospital stay and what led up to it — all of it has conspired to keep me from my digging into whatever lies beneath the facade of this strange little town. It's almost like I've gotten too close, and now the town itself, its people — hell, its animals — are trying to distract me from any further explorations. It would be very easy to get suspicious and fearful, but I'm determined not to let myself fall into that. I just tell myself I had too much time to think while I was lying around in my hospital bed.

Back to better thoughts: Patricia is getting a lot of information from different colleges and other schools in the mail. She wants to go to college this fall and become a nurse, but she's not sure about leaving her old grandma. We talked about that and, oh, about a lot of things — although, again, I didn't get near any of the stuff with the cats or the town or any of that. Something has kept me from asking her what she knows about it. Someday I imagine I'll have to, though, and maybe soon.

Anyway, Patricia brought me home yesterday morning. Ma had clean crinkly sheets on my bed, and I've never felt anything nicer. I've been sleeping most of the time ever since.

With Patricia and the folks from Mackaville dropping by the hospital, along with the calls from you and my parents, my spirits didn't have much of a chance to droop and I didn't feel a lot of "poor Robert," although I was in some pretty mean pain for the first few days. My left hand and arm were both swollen and black, and for a while there Dr. Jennings thought the venom had weakened my system so much that I was in danger of getting pneumonia or something else about as bad. I had to bunk at good old Dodd General until the swelling went down and I stopped peeing blood. Like I told you the other day, I'm damned lucky, or blessed, which like we've always said are two words for the same thing.

I hope you can read this handwriting ok. My typer's right there on the desk next to me, but I'm not quite able to get there yet. And I'm real tired. So more later.

Your thankful pal,

Robert

July 9, 1939
Sunday morning

Dear John,

Doing a little experiment while everyone's at church to see if I can sit up and type again, for the first time in what seems like forever. So far, my only ambulatory moments have involved shuffling down to the crapper in my pajamas, although I did manage to get a bath in yesterday afternoon. Ma is trying to see that I take it easy, doctor's orders, but I lie in bed and think about how far behind I'm getting in my interviews and wondering about everything I've seen since I've been in this place, and that makes me think of you and the letter I need to write you, and so now here I am, my bony carcass parked in my chair, clacking these typewriter keys I haven't touched for a couple of weeks.

I apologize if I told you on the telephone what I'm about to write — as you could tell, I was kind of punchy and befuddled the first couple of times you called — but now I'm ready to get down on paper exactly what happened. I knew, too, that the calls were costing you a lot, so I didn't want to go off on any long-winded tales.

On the other hand, it costs next to nothing this way — a little bit of typewriter ribbon, a few sheets of paper — and it's for the record. So here goes:

Monday morning, the day after I'd witnessed that unbelievable set-to between the hogs and the snakes (That'd be June 27, according to my desk calendar, and damn but that seems like a lifetime ago!) at the Gabbers', I headed out after breakfast to see if I could get an interview with a Mrs. T. C. Hardage, who, coincidentally enough, lived on another of those so-called Witch Mountains. I'd been on the road for I guess ten minutes and I was climbing a hill at a pretty good clip when I glanced over and saw Old Man Black's hat kind of working its way up out of the sidecar, a part of its weathered brim flapping in the wind. Truth to tell, I'd forgotten I'd stuck it in there after picking it up outside the Gabber's fence.

I was afraid it was going to fly out, so I reached over to stuff it down onto the floor of the sidecar.

That's when it struck.

I mean struck. That damned rattlesnake hat band done reared up with a big viper head and sank its fangs into my hand, one right into the knuckle of my thumb, the other through the web between thumb and forefinger. I swear, John, I could even hear its rattles buzzing above the noise of the Indian and the air rushing past.

The pain shot through my hand and up my arm like I'd grabbed a live electrical wire. I reacted without thinking, shaking my hand hard until the damned thing flew off, just a few seconds before I would've launched myself off the side of the mountain into space. The surprise and pain had made me swerve hard left and in a few more seconds I wouldn't have had to worry about the snake because I would've been a dead son-of-a-bitch well before the poison could kill me. Luckily, I was able to jerk the front wheel of the Indian back in line, horsing it around with my good arm, although I nearly jackknifed in the process. That's what adrenaline can do for you. Meanwhile, my left hand pulsed and ached and throbbed, the venom racing hotly through it and up my arm toward my heart. I could almost feel it moving in me.

I knew I was in deep shit. All I could think about was getting to Dr. Chavez as quickly as I could. So I did a U-turn and gunned the motor, heading back toward town. My hand was already starting to change color, and as I roared down the hills, weaving a lot more than I intended, I stuck my hand up to my mouth and sucked for all I was worth. I tasted venom and blood and I kept at it, sucking and spitting, until I wasn't getting anything at all. My head felt like a balloon some kid had let float away into the sky. I knew I should be cutting the fang marks to let the poison drain, but it would have been impossible to keep the Indian on the road and do that as well, and I had to get to the doc above all else.

I roared into town, increasingly woozy, and pulled up in front of the doctor's office. By this time, everything seemed to be pulsating around me, in and out, and the door to the office was all wavy lines. I remember stumbling in and almost falling, seeing the faces of the people in the waiting room, their mouths big O's as they gaped at me, and then the voice of Dr. Chavez. I think I said "snake," but I can't be sure. I vaguely remember him shouting something at his nurse about rubber tubing and I thought, "Why the hell rubber tubing?" and then I went out like a dead man.

That's what I'm going to do right now. Even though I've taken my good sweet time to type this, lying down for rest breaks three or four times, I feel like I've just run the Bunion Derby. But it's a good feeling, too, knowing I can still pound a typewriter.

More coming.

Exhaustedly,

Robert

July 10, 1939
Monday morning

Dear John,

I'm telling myself that I'm writing you this morning instead of going out on my job as an experiment, just to see if I've regained the stamina I need to write up my interviews. Really, though, I know I'm not going anywhere today. Probably tomorrow. I need one more day before I climb back onto my trusty Indian companion.

So instead of typing up one of the tales from the hill folk, I'll spin you my own yarn. It's one I should have sent you long ago, about Old Man Black and the cigarette butt.

I figure you've already guessed what I was doing, based on the clues I was giving you along the way, like Seth Black asking what I was doing to their Pa that day in Foreman's Drug Store, and what the sheriff said about the old man being down with a "sharp pain in his chest that won't go away." Of course, your sending the books I asked for was the most important thing about it all — that and the butt with Black's saliva soaked into it.

It was that Tuesday night I came back from Doctor Chavez's after having my stitches pulled. That'd be clear back to the 20th of June, exactly a week before I was hospitalized up in Harrison and ten days after my escapade with the rattler at the boarding house. I helped Pete out at the station until he closed up, and then I adjourned to my room and locked the door. MacWhirtle heard me come in and came up the stairs with me, but I told him I needed to be alone and shut the door on him. His whining told me he didn't understand, but he was too independent to sit there and protest for very long, and pretty soon I heard him slowly head toward the stairs.

It almost broke my heart to turn him away like that, but I had to. I didn't even want a dog as a witness. If I was determined to do this, and I was, then I was going to do it in secret.

I think I told you I'd bought some paraffin wax from Sparky Winters. He asked me if I was going to chew it, which is what I guess some of the kids do around here, and I told him no, I was getting it for Ma to can with. Hell, I've got no idea if anyone does any canning in the summer. But he bought it, I guess, because he didn't even lift an eyebrow.

Then again, there was no need for him to be suspicious. Even as enmeshed in the abnormal as this town is, I'll bet most of the population couldn't have known what I was going to do with the paraffin.

Of course, I could be wrong.

I did it that evening, in my locked room, taking a candle and heating up pieces of the wax until it was pliable enough to shape. Then, I fashioned a little paraffin man about four inches tall. When I had him put together, I heated up his back, pulled it apart down the middle, and laid the butt in like it was his spine. Then I covered it up and sealed it in.

Ma always had a basket of quilting scraps lying around in the living room, with pinking shears sitting on top. I hoped she wouldn't miss the little pieces of denim and cotton I'd snipped off after I'd gotten the idea to do what I was doing. The cloth could be made to stick to the wax, so I didn't really have to do much but cut it to shape with my pocket knife.

I don't think you need to know all the things I did, both before I started and as I was making and finishing off the doll. I'll just say that I followed the procedure laid out in Dr. Forebusher's Magic in the Islands, which was published in 1903 and is still the best and most complete book on voodoo, Seabrook's much more famous tome included. Again, I'll never be able to thank you enough for sending it and the other books I asked for from my shelf back home.

When I got through with the doll it looked pretty damn good, like a tiny, ugly, golem-like version of Old Man Black. I even had a little scrap hat for him. After admiring my work for a few moments, I reached for the hatpin I'd lifted from one of Ma's Sunday hats, peeled down the snippet of denim that covered the chest area of the doll, and heated the end of the pin in the flame of the candle until it smoked. Then I shoved it in.

I can't tell you if it was the seventh

sense, but I can tell you this: I'll swear I heard an old man scream then, horrid echoes ping-ponging through my head. A wave of nausea hit me and I almost threw up. Sweat was running into my eyes, and it wasn't from the heat outside. My heart thundered. The fact I was screwing around with something well beyond my understanding, something powerful and maybe truly evil, hit me unexpectedly hard.

I didn't stick the pin clear through. I just jabbed it in a little ways, twisted it around a little, and pulled it back out, leaving a black speck of soot to mark the tiny entry hole.

I considered whether to stick it in again, but something cautioned me not to. So I affixed the bit of denim back onto the doll's chest and wrapped the little effigy in a handkerchief of mine that was stiff and colored a rusty dull red with my own blood. Either Pete or I had used it to stanch my bleeding after our encounter in the hills, and I'd kept it in a drawer as a reminder of that day, I guess. Or maybe I somehow knew I was going to need it later, to follow the procedure laid out by old Dr. Forebusher. Magic in the Islands, you see, says that's the way to keep a spell active — by wrapping the effigy in something stained with the conjurer's own blood.

The conjurer. Damn. Is that what I am?

Anyway, I stuck the little package in my front pocket, determined to have it on me whenever I left my room, and right near me when I was in my room. If another rattlesnake showed itself, I was going to take that doll out and bite its head off.

On that I'll crawl back into bed and get some more rest. I plan to gin the interviews back up tomorrow so I'll be able to get done by my October 1 deadline. Given all that's gone on around me, I find it very funny that I'm supposed to light out of here the month of Halloween.

Your pal and faithful comrade,
Robert

July 12, 1939
Wednesday evening

Dear John,

I guess my conscience finally got to me. That's the only way I can explain not only what I did today, but also why I've included a little photo in this letter. And even though what I did cost me a half day that I can scarcely spare, especially after getting so behind while I was in the hospital, now I'm glad I did it.

(By the way, it looks like the WPA is going to pay my medical expenses, so once again God bless FDR and his alphabet soup.)

First of all, if you haven't been able to figure out that Old Man Black and his kids are no damn good and would gleefully gut me like a fat hog if they could, then you haven't been paying very close attention. Still, that old man's been suffering now for over a month. Despite myself, I sometimes wake up thinking about how the pain is with him always, no matter what he does, and it troubles me. Not to go melodramatic, but I now know what it's like to hurt continually and worry that it's never going to go away.

I've only been back doing interviews since yesterday, and I know I'd better light a shuck if I'm going to finish in my allotted time, but this morning as I rode off to still another shack in the hills, I couldn't shake the thought of what that old man was going through. So as quick as I got Miz Zella Roberson's reminiscences of her dear sweet gran'ma taken down in my notebook, I decided to drive the Indian into Harrison. I had an idea that might help both me and that snaky old murderous bastard.

There's a nice little penny arcade right next to the picture show in Harrison. I don't think I told you about it before, but Pete and Diffie took me by once on our way to the theater, and along with the test-your-strength machine and the girly-show Kinescopes that date back before the flapper era, there's a booth that'll give you a strip of four little photographs for a quarter. That's where I headed, me and Old Man Black's little lookalike.

I got in, closed the curtain, and pulled the doll from my front pocket, unwrapping the handkerchief from around it. Then I peeled down the front of the denim that served as its tiny overall bib so that the little chest hole showed. Taking a pencil out of that same pocket, I ran its lead around the pinprick, hoping I could get it dark enough to show up in a picture.

As you can see, I did. That little doll I'm holding up next to my cheek is the Black effigy I told you about. You don't have to look too hard to see that dark spot in the middle of his chest, do you? I don't imagine Old Man Black had to, either.

I'd brought an envelope from my room, and a

piece of paper. Sitting right there in the photo booth, I wrote:

"Mr. Black,

I hear you've had a pain in your chest for a few weeks now, and nothing seems to help. It may sound funny to you, but my little friend here has exactly the same problem. I haven't been in the best of health lately either, as you may have heard.

I'm feeling better now, and I think both you and my little friend will be feeling better by tomorrow. But if anything else bad happens to me, I think my little friend would be really torn up. He might even lose his head. And you might feel a lot worse too.

You can tell me how you're feeling tomorrow if you want to. Call me on the telephone at Ma Stean's. The number is 133. You don't need to come by, and don't send your boys or anybody or anything else. I'd hate to have a relapse, and I bet you and my little friend would hate it, too. It's good not to be in pain, isn't it?"

I signed the letter and put it in the envelope with a photo that showed the doll's chest to good advantage. Then, writing "Mr. Black" in big letters on the outside of the envelope, I left the place and headed for the hills.

Well, not quite. I felt so good that I stopped off at a second-hand store I'd passed on the way into town and bought a pair of worn but still good-looking dress shoes, a good white shirt, a black tie with fire plugs on it, black slacks, and a belt. I'd be lying if I told you I didn't get them mostly so I'd have something new to wear when Patricia and I went out. The CCC uniforms I'd been wearing ever since my days with that outfit were starting to get a little threadbare, so I also got a pair of railroad coveralls that were real cheap because they were pretty worn, a pair of big brown work shoes, brogans, and a beat-up old railroad-engineer's cap to top it all off. I figured going off to do interviews in that sort of getup might make me look less intimidating to the hill folk. Not that it's going to matter in a couple of months. In the mail this morning, along with the letter and forms from the WPA re: my hospital bill, was another official government letter telling me about my new job as a clerk-typist at the War Department. I'm to be assigned on Oct. 16 to a General Mason. Near as I can tell, they have in mind some use for my "compositional and translation ability." I think that means I will work on making stuff more understandable? Your guess is as good as mine at this point.

Back to Harrison. To be honest, one of the reasons I stopped at that place was the used bookstore I'd spied next door, and I could've spent every cent I had left in it. John, there were thousands and thousands of pulps in there, all in boxes and shelves and most of them a nickel each, even the ones with a July cover date. I didn't even get to the books, although

I will next trip. I allowed myself to spend three bucks, which got me enough bags of pulps to fill up my sidecar. Even if I were to go through one a day, I'd still have reading material for months to come.

The next part of the trip was the trickiest. I knew now exactly where the Blacks lived, but I also knew that every time I'd been around their place bad things had happened. I was convinced they had snake sentinels around there that somehow got the word to Old Man Black whenever I was in the area. Yeah, I would've called that notion batty a few months ago. I don't now.

I could've done the easy thing, gotten his address at the Mackaville post office and sent the photo and note as a letter, but I guess I wanted something more immediate. Plus, as I told you before, there's something about that Gibson, the postmaster, I don't like. I won't go so far as to say that he sets off my seventh sense, but I sure get uneasy around him. Maybe it's just the way he looks, with big high nostrils like Ernest Thesiger in The Bride of Frankenstein. He looks down over those nostrils at you, too, in a kind of condescending way. Not a pleasant gee to be around.

Anyway, instead of going by the p.o., I told myself I'd take the Indian up toward Black's and if I started feeling like something was about to happen, if my seventh sense kicked in at all, I'd turn back and forget it.

John, I don't know what I expected to feel

as I approached the Black place, but I felt nothing. The Indian was making the kind of dinosaur roar it always makes, and I was sure it would get their attention, but even when I stopped right at the rickety mailbox with "BLACK" painted on it, the big engine revving, I felt no sense of danger at all.

The weather-beaten house — a shack, really, that no self-respecting sharecropper would've lived in — stood back maybe a hundred yards from a broken-down fence by the road, the yard weedy and unkept, a few listless chickens pecking at it in the noonday heat. That old pick-up I'd seen Black in at Jolley's Mercantile was nowhere around, so maybe he was away and that's why I wasn't feeling any alarm. Even so, I still didn't waste any time dawdling. I stuck the envelope in the box and hauled my ass out of there.

When I got home, I unwrapped my "little friend" and, again going by Forebusher, took a candle to the doll's chest and melted down the spot where I'd stuck the pin, after first taking some rubbing alcohol from the bathroom cabinet and cleaning around the tiny hole. When I finished, it was smooth and unblemished as new flesh.

Now I'm sitting here in my room, half-expecting Ma to knock on my door and tell me I'm wanted on the telephone. Maybe I won't get any response at all from Old Man Black. Maybe he's too ignorant to connect the photo and the note with his loss of pain. Or, hell, maybe

it's all coincidental bullshit and I didn't
cause his chest pains at all. But I don't
really believe that. In fact, no matter how it
turns out, I feel happy and relieved, like a
weight's been lifted. I did the right thing.
I'm sure of it.

Now, I'm going to crack one of those pulps
I've piled up in my room and try and forget
about everything but the novel about this new
character called the Black Bat, running in
Black Book Detective. MacWhirtle's right here
on my bed, waiting for me to finish typing and
wagging his tail every time I look down at him.
He must know how good I feel.

Your pal and faithful correspondent,
Robert

July 15, 1939
Saturday morning

Dear John,

Oh, boy. Where do I start?

I guess I should say first that I got your latest letter and I'm glad you're still convinced I haven't gone around the bend. Now I'm going to tell you what's happened since I wrote you last time.

First of all, it was all quiet the evening I wrote you. With MacWhirtle lying contentedly next to me on the bed, I got through the entire Black Bat novel (not bad) and read all the stories in the back of the mag as well. Those few hours of losing myself in those pulpwood pages were just what I needed. When I got to the last story, I even took out that jar of corn-squeezin's from the Gabbers and took a little sip. One was plenty. I slept like a dead man.

The next morning, Thursday, I got a wild hair and dressed up in my new used railroad duds I got for cheap in Harrison before I headed out to the hills for my interviews. Funny enough, I really hit the jackpot with a family called the Woodruffs. Turns out they've had lots of railroaders in the family, so they took me in as one of them and among them gave me about a half-dozen stories I can use — colorful, but not weird, mostly about trains.

They even used some rail lingo I'm going to have to look up.

(A side note: Did the seventh sense tell me to wear the railroad-man clothes that morning, or was it just coincidence? After a couple of months in this town, I'm not sure anything is coincidence anymore.)

Coming down out of the hills after spending most of the day with various Woodruffs, I started thinking about Old Man Black and wondering why he hadn't called. That led me to think about his twin idiot sons and our last meeting, and by the time I'd made it in to Pete's station I admit I was a little worked up. I wouldn't have called it a premonition, exactly, but I was goosier than I thought. Toward closing time, I was sitting in Pete's swivel chair drinking a Coke and keeping an eye on the gas pumps while he rebuilt a carburetor for a Studebaker pick-up truck one of the Gabber clan had brought in. A car pulled in and, as the driver shut it down, it backfired. I threw myself over backward, banged my head and nearly broke my neck, and the Coke bottle came spiraling out the doorway to the bay and almost brained Pete.

"What the hell!" he hollered as he dodged the spewing missile.

I was more embarrassed than I was hurt, and by the time I got up and out to the pump, the lady could hardly stifle her laughter.

"My lands," she said, "I'm sorry. Are you all right?"

"Yes, ma'am," I returned, shamefaced.

"Then please fill 'er up." Looking over my shoulder, she sputtered as though she had a case of the church house giggles. I turned to see Pete, who'd come out of the station. He was laughing, too.

"You tryin' to kill my help, Mildred?" he asked her. He had tears in his eyes.

Great, I thought. Now everybody in town's going to think I'm a spook. I didn't say anything else while I filled up her auto, washed her windows, and checked her oil. Pete took her money. They both knew I was uncomfortable, so they tried not to laugh anymore, but they only partially succeeded. After she drove away, Pete told me he was sorry, but it was the funniest thing he'd seen in quite a while. Finally, I managed to smile about it, too, although my face hadn't quit burning. And I found myself still halfway looking out for Blacks.

When I got back to the boarding house, Ma was waiting for me at the door. Nodding at the other boarders behind her and at Patricia, who was setting the table in the dining room, she stepped out on the porch and shut the door.

"Need to talk about a coupla things," she said by way of preamble. "Just you 'n' me."

"Sure, Ma," I returned. And the seventh sense went off inside me like a burglar alarm.

"You got a call today, 'round noon. Didn't identify hisself, but he didn't need to. It was ol' man Black."

I reached down to pet Mac, who'd squeezed out the door just before Ma shut it. I was trying to be casual, but my heart was thundering.

"What did he say?"

"He asked for Brown. I told him you wasn't here. He said, 'Then tell him, "All right."' That's all he said. Didn't even say goodbye. Just hung up."

I nodded. "Okay. Thanks."

"Then them two Black boys was here askin' about you."

"When?"

"'Round three thirty. Said they wanted to talk and asked when you'd be in."

Three thirty was about the time I'd come down out of the hills full of the edginess I'd tried to tell myself was nothing.

"What did you tell them?" I asked.

"I said I didn't know." She looked out into the darkness. "They might come back tonight. They might not. I 'spect they'll be back around, though, and I just wanted to make you aware."

I could hear the muffled tones of Fred Waring's music on the living room radio. Ma Stean's eyes shone like a cat's in the gathering dusk.

"You wanna see 'em?" she asked.

"I don't know. I don't think so."

"Well, you could allus put the fix on 'em, like you did their daddy." She smiled a little — again, like a cat — and watched me.

"Ma!" I began. "What in the world gave you—"

"Shhhh!" she cautioned, looking back at the door.

I brought it down to a whisper. "What in the world gave you that idea?"

She put a big hand on my back. "C'm'on," she said. "Walls got ears."

With Mac tagging along at our feet, we stepped off the porch and walked down to the gate. It was almost dark now, and Ma looked around with those shining eyes before continuing our conversation.

"Folks know you gave him the miseries," she said. "They don't know exactly how, but they know it was you. The big question is how come you didn't come right out and <u>kill</u> 'im 'specially after he pret' near took your own life."

"You know he was responsible for that?"

"Sure." she said. "Ever'body does. And we're all just glad the doc up in Harrison pulled you through. Could've been plenty bad if you'd croaked — and not just for you."

John, you know how I am. I have never been too good at holding back how I feel, and when something's bedeviling me I want to get to the bottom of it. Unlike Jack, Doc, and Reggie, I don't love a mystery, and this town is the biggest mystery I've ever been involved in. To me, Ma's words sounded like the fuse that could ignite this whole mess and blow it sky-high.

"Ma," I said, trying hard to keep my voice down, "I didn't kill that old man because I don't want to kill him. I want him to leave me

the hell— excuse me, the heck alone, that's
all. I didn't really even want to hurt him, but
it seemed to me that was the only way to get
his attention. I just came here to do a job and
I'm trying as hard as I can to do it right and
completely before my time's up and I get sent
to Washington."

Ma nodded. "Shore," she said. "But—"

"Let me go on. I'll answer your question if
you answer mine. I know there's something that
runs deep through this town, right to its very
marrow. It has to do with cats and pigs and
snakes and all of you folks, or at least a lot
of you. Some of the best people I've found here
— you, and Mrs. Davis, and maybe even Pete —
seem to tie into the cats, and then there are
the Gabbers with their pigs and Old Man Black
and the rattlers." I was hissing like a
teakettle and I couldn't stop. "It's supernatural, Ma. I know that. I've told you and Mrs.
Davis about my seventh sense. But the seventh
sense won't tell me is how it all works, and
what it all has to do with something called the
Cleansing."

I couldn't tell for sure, but she seemed to
recoil a little when I said that. Even Mac
looked at me as though I'd said something he
didn't like. And all the time, my seventh sense
was ringing through me like a fire alarm.

"So," I concluded, feeling suddenly drained.
"What can you tell me?"

She took a deep breath and I thought for a
moment I was actually going to have this all

finally laid out in front of me. But then, she shook her head.

"We got rules, Robert," she said. There was a kind of sadness in her voice.

"Rules?"

She nodded.

"Rules, maybe, that keep you from doing anything about Black? I mean, you know that old bast— old guy keeps trying to kill me, and I'm pretty sure you like me all right, but I'm thinking maybe you could've done more to keep him and his snakes off me."

Again, Ma looked around, her eyes big in the dusk. When she spoke, it was barely a whisper.

"Robert," she said, "you're right about a lot of things — at least so far as it goes. But you're gonna be gone in a few months, and we're gonna be stayin' right here."

Someone else told me that, I thought. Then I remembered it was Sheriff Meagan, the night he took me to the doctor after the ambush in the hills.

"I understand," I whispered back. "I don't want to upset the applecart. I don't want to overturn the order of things in Mackaville. I just want to know what's going on around me."

About ten yards behind us, the front door opened, and a rectangle of light fell on the two of us and MacWhirtle. The figure in the doorway spoke tentatively into the darkness.

"Ma?"

"Be right there, Patricia," she said

briskly. Then, nodding her head at me, "C'm'on. Time ta eat."

"You going to tell me anything?" I whispered.

"Not yet. You done us a favor not submittin' them reports about colored folks and all, and we 'preciate it. You're a smart fella, smart enough to take on Old Man Black, so we 'spect you already know some 'bout it. And maybe you know <u>more</u> 'bout some other things, too — like how to put a <u>spell</u> on somebody."

She stopped as we reached the door, Patricia watching us with raised eyebrows. "Sorry, Ma," she said. "It's suppertime and I lost track of you."

"We was just havin' a conversation, child." She smiled. "I brought 'im back fer ya."

As dark-complected as Patricia is, her cheeks still flushed.

Much more later.

Your pal and faithful correspondent,
Robert

July 15, 1939
Saturday afternoon

Dear John,

I'm putting this letter in the same envelope as the one I wrote a few hours ago and that might be confusing so I'd better explain. Although I'm pretty much 100 percent cured, my pep isn't what it was before the hospital stay, so I just got tired and had to lie down for a while before I could finish all I wanted to write you. I slept hard until about 1 p.m., and now I'm up and at 'em and telling myself I'll head down to Castapolous's for a hamburger as soon as I finish giving you the story of my Thursday night. There's still a lot to tell, so I'll get right with it.

One of the reasons Patricia blushed at what Ma said to her is that we've made a practice of not acting like there's anything between us at the boarding house. We decided we just didn't want to be public about it. If one of the boarders sees us out at the movies or having a Coke at Foreman's, that's one thing, but there's no point in flaunting it. Patricia thought it would be inappropriate, and I agree. Ma of course knows what's going on between us, and I imagine Dave and Paul and Mister by-God Clark do too, but still...

Anyway, after supper I sat around in the living room for a little while, listening to the <u>Maxwell House Show Boat</u> when Mr. Clark wasn't interrupting it by railing about what the Republicans were trying to do to sabotage FDR, and how some of 'em had a lot in common with old Uncle Adolf over in Europe. Well, actually, I wasn't listening to either the radio or Mr. Clark as much as I was thinking what I was going to do if I heard a knock at the door, because I knew it would surely be the Blacks coming by again.

Finally, I got so jittery that I couldn't sit around anymore, so I excused myself and went up to my room. I was going to sit at my desk and type up a couple of reports, but then I got to thinking that if I turned the light on, I might be making myself a perfect target. To check out my theory, I put a pillow on the chair and snuck out the back door. Sure enough, a man who was good with a gun could easily have nailed me from the sidewalk.

Going back up, I made sure to stay away from the window and moved my bed until the head was out of any line of fire. That way, at least I could read.

I pulled up the window until a good breeze was wafting through, dug my H&R .22 out of its hiding place in the closet and put it on the table next to my bed, and then lay down and cracked into a <u>Private Detective</u> I'd picked up for a jit at that second-hand bookstore in Harrison. I'd just begun reading the first story when there was a knock at my door. I jumped up like I'd been popped with a whip.

Grabbing the revolver, I said, "Yeah?"

"Robert?" The voice was soft but unmistakable.

I opened the door. "Patricia," I said. "What are you doing here?"

She stood before me, uncertain and beautiful, like a butterfly about ready to dart away. Looking down the hallway, she whispered, "I just wanted to know if you were all right."

"Sure," I said.

"Good. I was here in the kitchen when those Blacks came by. I heard them call your name. Are they after you? Is that what Ma wanted to tell you tonight?"

Her eyes went to the pistol in my hand and then back to my face, and I grinned in what I hoped was a reassuring way. "Naw," I told her, "but in case they show up again, I figure this'll scare 'em off."

"All right." She didn't seem totally convinced. "I'm just worried some." Then, quickly, she kissed me on the cheek and went off down the hall to the stairs. I watched her leave, thinking that it had taken some guts to come right to my room, up here deep in male territory, and not worry about giving our little romance away to the boarders. I really liked her for that, and for a lot of other things, too.

I locked my door and headed back to bed, but I guess the fates were conspiring against my reading "Death on Display" by our favorite fictioneer Robert Leslie Bellem, because I'd no more than settled in again and scanned the first couple of paragraphs when I heard a noise outside. Peering out the window, I watched as the Black twins pulled up underneath a street lamp and got out of that old truck of their daddy's. Sam still had his arm in a sling, and Seth was tucking a six-shooter into his belt and pulling his shirt over it.

Well, John, in the seconds it took for them to walk around to the front of the house, a thousand things went through my mind. I was fairly sure they wouldn't try to pull any funny stuff on Ma or the rest of the boarders, and I told myself they'd better not try anything with Patricia. I knew they were here for one big reason, and that was to find me and avenge their dear old snaky daddy. So, making up my mind in a flash, I popped the screen latch, climbed out the window, crept to the overhang and let myself down until I was just holding onto the edge of the roof by my fingers. It still looked like a hell of a long way to the ground, but this was the course of action I'd chosen and it was too late to change now. So I dropped, hitting on my heels and rolling over backward, tumbling to a stop no worse for the wear. Jumping up, I made the shed in jig time, unlocked it, and kicked that old Indian to life.

Like I told you, I didn't think they'd start anything with anyone else in the house, but just in case, and because I knew Patricia hadn't had time to leave yet, I turned the Indian toward the street in front of Ma's and roared past, hollering, "Hey, Blacks — you goofs looking for me?"

They were still at the door when I passed, and it was almost comical to see them stumble off the porch toward their truck, each one trying to outrun the other, while Ma watched from the door. Over the roar of the motorcycle, I could hear Seth shouting at me, something about holding up.

Yeah. Fat chance.

I gave the bike the gas and let out the clutch, sending up a big rooster tail of gravel as I blasted onto the street and let 'er rip toward the highway. I figured my best chance was to head for some wide-open spaces so I could lose those clowns. When I turned right about three blocks later, I checked my little side mirror and saw the Blacks' truck barreling along in hot pursuit.

That was just about the time I remembered that in my haste to exit I hadn't picked up the pistol in my room. And my sawed-off shotgun was there as well, stuck in a closet where it couldn't do me a damn bit of good.

Well, it was too late now. Without Damon Runyon's "old equalizer" to fall back on, the only chance I had was to outrun them.

Shortly I was on the two-lane highway outside of Mackaville, and that's when I really opened her up. At full throttle, those four big cylinders really have an impressive growl. Taking the first turnoff, I headed right up into the hills. Of course, they knew this

territory better than I did, but I figured if I
could get a mountain curve or two between us I
could ditch 'em for sure. In a couple of
moments, Tolliver Road came up on my left. I'd
been over it several times to do interviews and
I knew it was steep and full of curves, so I
leaned over, took that corner at 60 miles an
hour, and started climbing and curving back to
the north, which was on my right. I kept the
bike opened up all the way, but the sidecar was
slowing me down. I could see in my mirror that
the Blacks were staying right with me, maybe a
half-mile or so behind.

The road climbed higher and higher, past
dark farms that were just lumpy shadows under
the bright gibbous moon. The REA hadn't made it
to this part of the country yet, so there were
hardly any lights anywhere. The beam from the
Indian's big headlamp bounced sideways against
a great rock cliff as I neared a long, somewhat
gentler stretch of road that I figured would
allow me to pull away from them. Then it would
be only a short pull to the crest, and once I
got over that they'd never catch me. I could go
down that mountain road at fifty or sixty miles
an hour, "rimming" like I wrote you about, and
they couldn't begin to stay with me unless they
wanted to shake that old truck apart.

Trees like dark sentinels flashed by me on
my right, and on my left a really spectacular
moonlit vista opened up as I headed for the
home stretch. Roaring around the bend toward
the crest, I suddenly slowed in unbelieving

dismay. Ahead of me, moving like bugs in the lantern-lit night, a big work gang of convicts in leg chains completely blocked the road, using shovels to spread a huge dump-truck load of gravel across it. I ground to a stop, the Indian rumbling in protest underneath me.

"Sorry, son," came a voice out of the darkness.

I looked over to see a fellow I figured was the road captain. He had a shotgun and a lantern, and he sat down the former and kept the latter while he shook a Lucky out of a pack toward me. I said no thanks.

"We're workin' 'em nights," he said, nodding toward the prisoners. "More humane than workin' 'em in th' heat, warden claims. Cain't let ya through right now. Oughta be done in 'bout half an hour though. Jest light an' relax 'til then."

I gave him what I'm sure was a sick grin, my mind buzzing. Trapped between a sheer drop on one side and a perpendicular sheet of rock on the other, I had a quick decision to make. Should I try to pick my way through that work party to the other side, and maybe get shot, or at least arrested? Should I stay where I was, taking a chance on the Blacks not shooting because of the lawmen with the work party? Or should I turn around and try to pop past the Blacks before they had time to blast me?

I chose the latter, turning around and starting back down toward the curve I'd taken about a quarter of a mile back, going back past the trees again — which gave me an idea. Maybe I could take to the woods and lose them that way.

When the Blacks' truck came roaring around a bend a few hundred feet ahead of me, the thought became action. Otherwise, I knew, I'd be trapped like an animal. It was even too late to try to reverse course and get back to the chain gang site. They'd have too much of a chance to pick me off from behind.

I shut the engine off, killed the light, slammed on the brakes, and steered with a thump into a bar ditch, where I leapt from the still-moving Indian and took off running as hard as I've ever run in my life, up the mountain, weaving in and out of the trees. Although there was decent moonlight, it was still dark enough for me to not see plenty of limbs, which slashed at me as I raced by. Once, I plowed right into the trunk of a big elm tree, which took me to my knees. But then I heard a yell from below and behind me and that got me to my feet and sprinting up the mountain again. Even though it was all uphill, I was making pretty good time, especially after I got a second wind. The more space I could put between the Blacks and me, the less chance they had of nailing me with whatever arms they happened to be toting. To make me an even more difficult target, I kept zig-zagging as I ran.

I was doing just fine until I hit the ravine.

It came up out of nowhere, about fifty feet

across and so deep that the moonlight didn't go all the way down. Still, in a wink I was sliding down into that darkness on my backside, bumping down rocky, loose soil until I'd slid to the bottom. It was a pretty long haul, 30 feet or so, but I made it in a hurry. In a moment, I was on my feet, hustling down the middle of the draw. There was enough of a glow there that I could pick out most of the obstacles in my path, although an outcropped rock sent me sprawling a time or two.

About a half-mile down, the draw started narrowing and suddenly I was at the end. Over my head about twenty feet was the lip of the waterfall that was barely trickling now but had once been responsible for creating the ravine. It was too tall and overhung for me to use it as a way of getting up and out. So, turning, I started retracing my steps, and I hadn't gotten very far when I realized I'd neatly sacked myself in. At this point, I had no idea where the Blacks were, but if they found me in this ravine I'd be a fish in a barrel. They could take their own sweet time to pick me off, and if I knew them like I thought I did, they'd probably make my agony last a long time.

I had to find a way to climb out, and since the walls were almost vertical and the soil loose, it was going to be a real challenge. I slowed and started pacing, looking for something that might help me get away. At least there was enough light to see my surroundings, even though clouds scudded periodically in

front of the moon, plunging everything into
momentary darkness.

It was just after one of these short-lived
blackouts when I spied a huge slab of rock that
had broken off from the rim and tumbled into
the ravine who knows how many years ago. It lay
tilted against the left bank, with its top only
six feet or so from the lip of the draw. Not
the perfect means of egress, but the best I had
with time of the essence, so I took a breath,
ran up the slab and jumped and caught the lip.
Luckily, I grabbed rock instead of loose soil,
and I began to chin myself up. If I'd been
fresh it would've been a snap, but as it was
I'd only pulled up chest high before I began to
feel myself falling back.

There was a little bush growing out on the
lip and I grabbed it with my left hand and
began pulling myself toward it. Clods of dirt
began rolling down toward me, and I prayed the
shrub's roots were deep enough, because if I
dropped back onto that tilted sandstone slab
there wouldn't be anything I could do to keep
from bouncing to the bottom of the ravine onto
the shards of rock that lined its floor.

Pulling myself up by the shrub, I let go of
the rock lip with my right hand and grabbed for
a little pine tree just beside it. Then I
pulled with both arms as hard as I could, and
once my belly button got even with the rim I
knew I was safe. I swung my legs up and rolled
over onto the flat rock — which suddenly
shifted with a cracking sound underneath me.

Leaping up, I plunged into the woods again, heading uphill, angling over toward the top of the cliff above the road. From there, I knew I could see the whole mountainside. Maybe I'd get lucky and spot the Blacks.

The trees got thinner, big tall pines mostly, and I slowed from a trot to a steady fast walk. The cool wind blowing in from the north felt good against my sweaty skin. Pretty soon, I could see the top of not only the mountain, but also the cliff I'd passed earlier, the one that faced the road. I stood in a spot where there was a lot of rock showing through the soil, the mostly barren landscape strewn here and there with lightning-blasted trees whose wood showed dead and white in the moonlight. It was like being in a graveyard, and for a moment I had a vision of the Mackaville cemetery and the group headstone and the cats. I moved quickly out of there and made my way to a big rock outcropping. Dropping to my stomach, I crawled cautiously out toward the edge, knowing that the lip of a cliff can be rotten and break with no warning. This rock, though, seemed solid, with no cracks that I could see.

I peered over and sure enough, there, far below me, was the road. I was dismayed to see that the road gang had packed up and gone. Had I been out here that long? Looking at my strap watch for the first time in a long time, I saw it was a little after 10 p.m., so I'd been gone from Ma's a little over two hours.

I thought about all of this as I reconnoitered, spotting the Blacks' truck and, not far from it, the ass end of the Indian, sticking out of the tree-lined ditch. If I could just stay out of sight until they left, I would be home free. Even if they wrecked my bike, Mackaville was only a three-hour hike, and — as long as they didn't haul the bike off or destroy it completely — Pete and I could come out later and tow it in.

I hadn't been there long at all, stretched out there on my stomach, watching and thinking, before I heard the sizzle of a striking match behind me. Whirling around, I saw the two Blacks, sitting on a log and leaning up against a big boulder. Seth was torching a cigarette. Sam had a rifle crooked in his good arm, pointed right between my eyes.

"Took ya long enough to git here," Seth said, grinning his snaggletoothed grin. He stood up, a revolver in his hand. Sam made a noise that sounded like a hiccup. I think he was laughing.

"Get up, Dan'l Boone." It was Seth again, motioning at me with the revolver and talking around his cigarette. "We been sittin' here a-listenin' to ya thrash through these here woods like some kinda fat blind hog. Ourselves, we come up th' trail." He pointed with his revolver to a clear footpath disappearing off down the hilltop.

I pushed myself to my feet. "That would've made it a lot easier for me," I said.

"<u>Wouldn't</u> it of, now?" said Seth. Sam clambered to his feet, making another noise that might've been laughter.

This was it, I thought. Two calm dumb killers in front of me, both with weapons, and a drop of hundreds of feet behind me. I knew I couldn't talk myself out of this one. Shake hands with the minister, Robert, because church is out for you.

Then, Sam spoke for the first time. "Ya wanna mess with 'im a little more 'fore we git to it?" he asked his idiot brother.

Seth continued to regard me with sinister amusement. "Aw, nah," he said after a moment. Then, to me: "It's like this. We wanna know if you'll kill our daddy fer us."

John, I've been at this for a couple of hours now, and reliving this little adventure has both revved up my appetite and tired me out. I promise to write tomorrow with the rest of it, but now that you know I didn't die and I've given you the twist in the story, I hope you can wait another day or two before getting the rest of it. I've got a burger to eat and a beautiful girl to take to the movies tonight, and I'm <u>bushed</u>.

Your pal and tuckered correspondent,

Robert

July 16, 1939
<u>early</u> Sunday morning

Dear John,

The sacrifices I make for you. Dawn has barely cracked, and here I am at the typer, writing down the rest of my confrontation with the Blacks because I promised you I would do it. It may be a little breathless because I have to get to church with Ma, Mrs. Davis, and Patricia in a couple of hours and after that who knows when I'll get back home. Mrs. Davis has really been putting on the Sunday dinner feedbag for me, and I probably overstay my welcome because I want to be around Patricia as much as I can. I've really fallen hard for her.

But that's a story for another time, and so are my observations about how well Tim McCoy is holding up as a western star. (Patricia and I saw one of his Bill Carson pictures, <u>Outlaw's Paradise</u>, last night.) Instead, here's the rest of the skinny on my tete-a-tete with the Black boys.

Seth's saying what he said there on the hilltop caught me completely off guard, as you might imagine. I stood there, every sense tingling, seeing and hearing and smelling to a heightened extent because until that moment I had believed I was going to be killed. The air had a fresh new smell. I could hear the labored breathing of the Blacks, the intake of smoke into Seth's lungs. I could hear my own heartbeat. For a moment, I felt like I was somehow more aware of all that was around me than a human being could be. I know it sounds nutty, but it was an animal awareness and I know it was because I'd thought I was a dead man.

Seth's gruff voice pulled me out of my reverie. "Well, how 'bout it?" he asked. "Hell, ya don't, he'll kill <u>you</u>, an' that's fer damn sure. This way, we can kinda set 'im up fer ya."

"Yeh," Sam chimed in. "We kin warn ya if'n he tells us any plans he's got fer ya.' "

They both paused, watching me. I was thinking hard about what I could — or <u>should</u> — say. Licking my lips, I plunged in.

"Fellas, I can't promise you I can kill your father. I mean, just because—"

That's as far as I got, because Seth had raised his pistol and Sam had clicked the safety off his rifle.

"I done <u>tole</u> you," Seth said, menace under the words, "If'n ya don't kill <u>him</u>, he's a-gonna kill <u>you</u>. Nex' rattler might bite ya in th' face, or th' throat, or maybe even right on th' enda yer pecker. Think you'd get <u>over</u> that?"

Sam made that hiccuping noise again. He was enjoying this.

"If you ain't smart enough to see you gotta kill 'im, we might as well blow yore ass off this cliff and go on back home. He might treat us good fer a while if'n we did ya in."

Just like that day when I'd been caught by

the Gabbers, I sent up a kind of lightning-bolt prayer that whatever came out of my mouth next might be the right thing.

"I didn't say I couldn't get him out of the way," I said quickly. "You can see I've got the power to do it. But how come you two want him gone?"

A look passed between them, and Seth threw his cigarette down and ground it out. "Ain't hardly none of yer bizness," he said, "but I'll tell ya anyways. We got us a half-brother, lot older'n us, down in Mississippi, there on th' coast. He's makin' good money, workin' in th' ship yards at a place called Pasca-goola. He wrote us a letter, said me and Sam could do it, too. Make good money, get drunk when we want, find us some wimmen. Do what _we_ want to do fer a damn change and quit workin' that goddamn old hardscrabble farm."

Sam spoke up then. "That old sumbitch won't let us go. Long as he says no, we gotta stay, and I'm fed up with his ol' ass. He been doin' this to his boys for th' past damn hundret years."

I stood there, stunned. A hundred years? Could he be <u>that</u> old? It'd explain a lot, if you believed in magic. And as far as I was concerned, if you had half a brain you couldn't live in Mackaville and <u>not</u> accept the super-natural.

"We seen that picture you sent 'im," Seth said. "That's how come we knew it was you what did it — 'specially after he got better an' full of ol' Nick again."

"You a conjure man," added Sam. "You what we need to put that ol' bastard in th' ground fer good."

I thought a moment. John, I've never killed anyone in my life, and the way I saw it, Old Man Black and I had come to an agreement to leave one another alone. But then again, how good is any deal you make with a snake?

"Tell you what, men," I said. "I think I can help you, but it's going to take a few days."

John, I was just buying time at that point. I didn't want to lie, but I didn't know if I could for sure kill a man, even one as foul and dangerous as Old Man Black.

Then, Seth did something that surprised me. He flipped his gun over and handed it to me, butt first. I could see what it was — an 1874 Colt Cavalry Revolver, .45 caliber. It's a hell of a weapon. But as soon as I took hold of it, the seventh sense shot through my whole body like fireworks. I knew that revolver was evil, even before Seth said, "It come outta th' house. Ol' man's killed plenty with it. Now, you use it to kill <u>him</u>."

I started to say that wasn't the way conjure men worked, but since saving my ass was still paramount in my mind, I let it go. Sticking the Colt in the pocket of my railroad overalls, I nodded.

"I'll be in touch with you fellas," I said.

"Right now, I'm ready to take that trail back home."

"Yeh," Seth grunted, and I followed him and his brother down the hill and all the way back to the Indian and their truck without another word being said.

That's it for right now. If one of her boarders goes to church, Ma fixes breakfast for him, and I can smell mine now.

More later from your pal and faithful correspondent,

Robert

July 18, 1939
  Tuesday evening

Dear John,
   Ever since the Black twins braced me about
getting rid of their evil dad I've been on the
brink of one of those periods where I cannot
shake a feeling of doom or depression. I don't
know how much of this is the seventh sense and
how much is the news from overseas, which is
inescapable. A month or so ago, Pat and I saw a
newsreel at the Palace about Hitler and
Mussolini and their "Pact of Steel," and ever
since then I've had a bad feeling that the
world's going to burst into flames any time
now. Although Pete's hard to read, I believe he
feels the same way. We talk about current
events a lot, and so do the other boarders at
Ma's, although Ma herself tends to stay out of
the discussions. Patricia doesn't say much
about it, either, but when she does, whatever
she says shows that she's been giving it some
serious thought. It's something else I like
about her. Still waters run deep and all that.
   Then, there's a more practical reason I'm
uneasy: I have no reason to believe that Sam
and Seth Black are paragons of patience and
self-restraint, and I keep thinking they're
going to show up here anytime and demand an
answer about whether or not I'll get rid of
their old daddy for them.
   I've been going over and over it in my mind.

Could I do it? God help me, when I think of the rattlers Old Man Black has sent my way, including that cute-trick hat band that damn near landed me on a slab, I feel like I could stand toe-to-toe with him and smile roguishly as I plunged a saber into his guts. But I know that's just bullshit. Like Mr. Castapolous told me this morning, once you look in the face of someone you've just killed, you carry their eyes with you forever.

It was Mr. Castapolous who gave me the idea to do what I'm getting ready to do. For the past couple of mornings I've been starting out very early, even before Ma gets breakfast on the table, and riding out to the farthest reaches of the county, seeing people on my list who live in places I haven't seen before. I tell myself I'm doing this so I can be on the road before this damned Arkansas heat starts baking the hills, but if I wanted to be brutally honest, maybe I'm getting out so that I won't be on the premises if the Black boys happen to show up early. Of course, if they wanted me, all they'd have to do is wait around Pete's or Ma's any evening. So far, they haven't.

Anyway, I was rolling through town about 4:30 this morning, past the couple of blocks of dark little storefronts, when I saw a light go on at the Castapolous Cafe. It turned out that Mr. E.V. Castapolous was just opening up his doors, earlier than anyone else in downtown Mackaville. I couldn't help but stop.

I've written you about Mr. Castapolous. He's a short stocky Mediterranean type, about the same age as our dads, who still has a faint accent, even though he came to Mackaville nine years ago, after working back East, and opened this little combination lunch counter, bar & grill, and Italian restaurant. (He was brought up in Italy — Italian mother, Greek daddy.) He always seems like he's glad to see me, and the feeling's mutual. This morning, he grinned and waved me in, started the coffee pot going, and before I could decline it he had an omelet sizzling on the grill.

I sat down on a stool at the counter, and as often happens, we started talking about events in Europe, and after he got through cussing his fellow World War I veteran, Benito Mussolini, he started talking about being a fighter pilot in the Corpo Aeronautico Militare, the Italian Air Force, flying mostly Nieuport 27s until the very end of the war, when he flew SPADs. I knew a little about his air-war background from previous conversations we'd had, but I didn't know, as he put it, "At armistice, I was the only fella left — only one out of all the fighter pilots I come up with."

He flipped the omelet and threw a couple of pieces of bread on the grill beside it. "I got very good vision 'n' I can see outta the corners of my eyes real good," he said, his back to me. "Always knew when a Heinie got on my tail. Our planes wasn't as good as the Albatrosses they flew, but ours was a lot more nimble and I could most always flip or dive outta th' way. Not always, though."

Turning from the grill, he walked up to me and bent his head down so I could see the long ridge of scar tissue just below his ear, receding into his hairline. I'd never noticed it before.

"Fella, he almost blow my brains out," he said, patting the scar. Then he straightened. "Some time I show you the holes he leave in my side and back. I flew home very quickly from that one, just set the bus down an' pass out, but not before I got 'im. Like I say, I got good eyesight. He was looking at me when he died. Sometime I still see his eyes; they stay with me always. Coffee's ready."

He put a steaming cup of java in front of me, where it was presently joined by a plate nearly running over with a giant omelet, grilled toast on the side. In the few seconds of silence while he hustled up my breakfast, I saw eyes myself, Old Man Black's eyes, narrowed and reptilian. Not the kind I'd want to tote around with me forever.

"You goin' back up inna hills this morning?" he asked, sipping from his own coffee cup.

"Yeah."

"You work awful hard."

"There's a lot to get done," I said.

"I know. Me, too. Open up at five a.m., don't close sometimes until midnight or after. I love it, but sometimes I just gotta lock up the place and get away for a couple days, out in the fresh air and sunshine, clear my mind."

Suddenly, it struck me that E.V. Castapolous was a very wise man. Getting away for a few days and letting my mind clear sounded like the best thing in the world for me to do right now. Even with my hospital stay, I'd managed to stay ahead of schedule on my interviews, and if I kept going at my present pace I'd be done well before deadline. So why not go out in the mountains somewhere, a place where neither the Black boys nor anyone else could find me, and dope things out on my own?

"When you get away, Mr. Castapolous, where do you go?" I asked. "Somewhere around here?"

"Oh, yah. Get off by myself. Hunt deer."

Then he started telling me about a cave he'd found on his last trip, and as he talked, I grew more excited about the prospect of seeing it for myself. At one point, I even got the survey map out of the sidecar and brought it in so he could show me the approximate location and give me a few landmarks.

He'd been on the trail a day and two nights, closing in on a trophy buck (whose stuffed head now stares down from above the cash register in the cafe, right next to the stuffed owl). As he worked up a stream, he spotted an unusual wall of stone atop the steep side of a canyon about fifty yards from where he stood on the creek bottom, and the sight intrigued him enough that he climbed up to get a closer look. Turns out the wall was made up of mortar-covered rocks.

He walked the length of it, peered around, and
saw, maybe 10 feet behind the wall, an opening
about four feet square, which he ducked his
head into. And John, it turned out to be a
good-sized cave, hidden away up there behind
the rock-and-mortar wall, with a spring issuing
from a back wall and running across the floor
to a hole in the front and down to the main
creek. The channel, he could see, was man-made,
and there was enough rotted wood around for him
to deduce that there had once been a crude roof
between the wall and the cave opening.

"I went in a little ways," he said, "and I
saw more wood piled up around the walls. I
didn't touch none of it. I don't b'lieve in
touchin' dead people's stuff. And it was cold
as th' grave in there. Gimmie th' jeebies.

"I ain't told no one else about it," he
said, taking a long drink of coffee. "I love
'em in this town, but they got their secrets,
y'know, and this could be one of 'em. Maybe
they don't want no foreigner nosin' into it."

"Maybe not," I said. "But I'm a foreigner,
too, in a way, and what you just described
sounds like Eden to me."

He shrugged. "No Eve," he said. "But suit
yourself."

No Eve, and no Patricia, I thought. That's
too bad. But no Blacks, no mysteries swirling
around me — no war news. That's good. That's
what I need.

"Thanks, Mr. Castapolous," I said, laying a
dollar bill on the counter.

"Sure," he said, and he ambled off to the register. I slipped past him while his back was turned and was out the door before he rang me up. As far as I was concerned, what I'd gotten from him that morning was worth every cent, and a hell of a lot more.

Your pal and faithful correspondent,
Robert

July 20, 1939
Thursday evening

Dear John,

Well, by damn, I've done it.

Three people — four, if you count Mr. Castapolous, whom I haven't officially told because I don't need to — know I'm heading out to the wilderness, and they're all sworn to secrecy. Only Mr. Castapolous knows exactly where I'm going. Pat and Ma and Pete just know I won't be around for a few days. They're the people I had to tell, and while I don't know if they understood it or not — especially Patricia, who looked so sad-eyed at me that I wanted to hold her tight for a long while and explain it had nothing to do with her — they're my friends, so they went along with me, or pretended to. I promised them all I'd tell them about it later, and assured Pete I would make up any time I'd lost helping him at the station.

I didn't lie. I just told them I was going to have to be away. I supposed I could've said the government called me to Little Rock or some such thing, but Ma would've known that was b.s. because she'd seen the stuff I was packing, like that waterproof silk eight-foot square ground sheet I'd gotten from Abercrombie & Fitch — the light tarp I think I wrote you about. I'm glad I brought it with me to Mackaville. It folds up to the size of a book, so it didn't take up much space in my suitcase, and back a lifetime ago when I was leaving Minnesota I thought maybe I'd need it in my new surroundings. Seventh sense? Maybe, because I've got a real feeling it's going to come in handy now. So will my Abercrombie & Fitch rain jacket, made of the same thin material as the groundsheet. I've packed it along with my browse bag and other essentials — strong twine, waterproof matches, a small cooking pot and utensils, compass, etc. — and that A&F stuff adds hardly any weight at all.

One interesting and important thing I've acquired is a no-batteries-needed flashlight I found for sale out at Dill Jolley's place. It's a funny kind of thing, with a clockwork-driven dynamo in it, like what Doc Savage uses. You wind it up and it runs for three or four minutes, then you have to wind it up again. Old Dill had just gotten a few in — who knows how, or from where — and he was very proud of 'em. I didn't bring up the fact that they were marked "Made in Germany," and neither did he. Probably the last thing I'll ever buy from that country.

When I was laying in supplies that I needed for the trip, I got some from one store and some for another, so it wouldn't look too suspicious. No sense in telegraphing how long I'll be gone — or that I'll be gone at all. So from Winters' Market I got a can of bacon, some powdered eggs, a good chunk of hard cheese, and four of those big Baker's chocolate bars, along with raisins, dried prunes, sugar, a bag of coffee, and a couple of small cans of condensed milk. These were exactly the kinds of foodstuffs a camper would take to the mountains, but if Sparky suspected that's what I was doing he kept it to himself.

The same day I got the flashlight at Jolley's Mercantile, I also bought some prospector's biscuits — just hard bread, really, or big crackers — along with four tins of sardines and some summer sausage, which Dill insisted I taste before I bought any of it. He was a little snoopier than Sparky, but I just told him I had some people to interview who were a long way out in the hills, and I might get hungry before I could get home. That seemed to satisfy his curiosity.

Another curious chap was Mr. Foreman, after I went into his drug store and asked him if he had anything that would kill the germs in creek water. Looking at me kind of funny, he said, "What would you want something like that for?"

"Well," I said, lying heartily, "my job takes me all over the hills and 'way out where there's hardly any civilization. In this summer heat, I drink a lot of water, and sometimes my canteen runs dry. I'd like to be able to fill it at a stream and not have to worry about getting sick from it."

He nodded, walked a little ways down, and reached under the counter, coming up with a bottle of iodine.

"Here you go. Eight drops of this to a quart of water, and you ought to be safe." He grinned. "Of course, it'll taste like the very devil, but it won't hurt you."

Thanking him, I gave him a dime for the bottle and left. I was just revving up the Indian to head back to Ma's when, down Main Street, I saw Mr. Castapolous come out of his store and wave at me, indicating he wanted me to come by. I guess people can recognize me now by the sound of the big motorbike.

I cut the engine and walked the half-block to his cafe. He seemed all buzzed about something.

It was around two p.m., so his lunch crowd was long gone, and most of the patrons coming in for a beer or dinner wouldn't be around for several more hours. Still, I was surprised when he hung a "closed" sign on the door and started pulling down all the shades.

"I got something to loan you," he said. Even though we were the only two people in the place, he spoke sotto voce. "I don't want folks to know what it is, or where it came from."

"Sure," I told him, having no idea what he was talking about.

Pulling down the last shade, he turned around, his eyes sparkling in the dusk-like interior of the place. "You still goin' out in th' hills, ain'tcha? Look for my cave?"

I grinned in spite of myself. "Sure, Mr. Castapolous, but don't let it get around, huh?"

"Sure." He grinned back. "I knew first time I tol' you 'bout it, an' you got out that map, you'd have to go see for y'self. Okay, then. Wait right there."

He scurried into the back and presently came out with a short carbine in a leather cover.

"This weapon here," he said, passing it to me, "she's a Mannlicher-Schonauer. 1910 made."

I took it.

"Brought with me from Italy," he said. "Big-game rifle — 9.5 x 57mm Mannlicher. You could kill a lion with her."

While I'd heard about those weapons over the years, this was the first I'd actually seen. It was littler than I figured it would be, just over two feet long and very lightweight. The wooden stock ran all the way up to the barrel, which was only a couple of feet long.

"A lion?" I asked. "With this?"

Mr. Castapolous laughed, pulling something from a white box. It was a shell about as long and big around as your index finger. "You don't know nothing, kid. Shoot this bullet, it knock you on your ass, and I ain't kidding. You tell me you shoot a Winchester? This one, she kick twice as hard. May look small, but she's a big gun. Look her over."

I turned the rifle over in my hands. It looked almost new.

In a moment, Mr. Castapolous returned, setting an ice-cold bottle of Chubby Lager on the counter in front of me. He swigged from another one, wiping the foam from his mouth with the back of a stubby hand.

"Bought 'er back when I was spoiled rich

brat, in the old country b'fore the war," he said, nodding at the Mannlicher. "There, I hunt wild boar and red deer. Taken some deer here with her, too — like that one." He gestured with his bottle at the head over the cash register, then drank from it again.

"You see, she's a beautiful gun. Silver front sight you can see inna dark, big rear sight, go into action quick, you bet. I'll give you about 50 shells so you can do a little practice shootin' if you want."

"Well, sure — and thanks, Mr. Castapolous," I said. "But—"

He cut me off. "I loan her to you 'cause you might need her. There ain't just deer up in them ridgebacks. Some of the ugliest boars I ever shot, too, an' it was self-defense. They'll come right for you, and you better be ready no kidding. This gun, she knock 'em over ever' time."

I worked the action, checked the sights, practiced throwing it up to my shoulder. After watching me silently for a few moments, Mr. Castapolous nodded his approval.

"Remember, now, she kick like a son-of-a-bitch. Get into them boars, though, you won't feel it." He grinned.

"Mr. Castapolous... I don't know what to say. I'll take very good care of her, of course. But I'm sure those shells are expensive. I'll be happy to pay you for—"

Again, he interrupted me, putting up a hand. "All the payment I need is for you to bring her

back in one piece. And you come back in one
piece, too, if you can."

Those last few words chilled me a little,
but I forced a smile.

"I'll be back in one piece, with a full
report," I told him. "And if I find any interesting relics, I'll share 'em with you."

"Good enough," he said, reaching for the
rifle. I handed it to him and he slid it back
into its case, which I noticed had a sling I
could use to carry it, even though I'll bet it
didn't weigh ten pounds.

"Bring the bike around back," he said. "I'll
wait there."

That was a good idea. It was too early for
deer season and, you know, people around here
are damned "funny" about hogs and pigs, so
keeping the rifle under cover seemed like a
damn good idea. I didn't want to be answering
any questions about the new weapon, so I pulled
around there, we loaded it into the sidecar,
covered it up and shook hands, and I was off,
feeling just a little more secure about my
trip.

This all happened only a few hours ago. I've
been getting lucky with the interviews, finding
almost everybody left on my list so far avail-
able and willing to talk. (As of today, I'm
down to a little more than thirty names, something that seems downright amazing to me.) This
morning, before I headed into town to get the
rest of my supplies, I talked to members of
four different families. The best story I got

was from a 94-year-old codger named Ezekiel Andras, who told me about the renegades who'd holed up in the mountains around here after the War Between the States and swooped down to loot and pillage the area farms. He said they'd also made blood money by catching and returning former slaves that had gotten away from the Indian tribes. It's a story I think might somehow fit into the puzzle of this place.

So I've got a lot to type up, which I'll do tonight. I already know I'll be too full of energy and anticipation to sleep very much, but I'm hoping the work will tire me out. If it doesn't, I'll try my usual insomnia remedy: a glass of milk, a few cookies, and a couple of Dan Turner, Hollywood Detective pulp stories, perchance to dream of Turner and those Tinseltown babies.

I take off before dawn tomorrow, heading west and slightly south of Mackaville with about 30 miles to cover before I get in the vicinity of Mr. Castapolous's cave. Then I'll find a place to park the bike well off the road, cover it, load up, and start marching. If I've calculated right, I'll have to cover about 10 miles of mountain country before getting to the cave. If I can just get through tonight without the Blacks showing up or anything else happening to disturb my plans, I'll be putting my groundsheet down in Mr. Castapolous's cave by this time tomorrow, give or take a couple of hours, away from this constant tension I've been feeling, ready to try and dope some things out.

John, there aren't any post offices or mail-boxes where I'm going, so you won't be hearing from me for several days. I'll take lots of notes so I can fill you in when I get back.

Of course, if for some reason I don't return, you know and my folks know you can have all of my books and pulps you want, and anything else of mine, too. I don't want to be melodramatic, but if something happens to me, I'm counting on you to keep my memory alive.

Your faithful correspondent and forever pal,
Robert

July 21, 1939
Friday night

Dear John,

I really <u>really</u> hope that you get this, and that it's the top sheet on a big thick stack of journal entries that you've pulled out of a package I mailed you. I'm taking extra precaution to make my handwriting clear and legible so that you can read it, and if you <u>are</u> reading it, that means I made it back to Mackaville and sent it all to you. I know you'll keep it in a safe place, along with the rest of my letters. I'll tell the world I think it could be a book someday.

I also admit that I'm writing this as legibly as I can because there's a fair chance, I guess, that something is going to happen to me out here, and if these notes survive and someone comes along — maybe soon, maybe years from now — they'll be able to make some sense of my demise. Not to be morbid. Just realistic.

So here goes:

This morning, leaving the Indian well-hidden in a big patch of woods a couple of hundred yards off a dirt road, I struck out across the hills looking for the landmarks Mr. Castapolous and I had marked down on my survey map. I didn't realize how much tension I'd been under until I walked away from the bike and the woods closed around me. In my mind, Arkansas isn't as pretty as our own state, but I have to admit

those ridges with their thick, cool greenery
had their own kind of beauty. Plus, they helped
me realize I was getting away from it all for a
while, away from Mackaville and the Blacks and
the ineffable strangeness that radiates from
every inch of that town — strangeness I've come
to accept as part and parcel of my daily life.
With each step, I felt lighter, as if the
weight of my worries was slowly evaporating
into the leafy branches of the trees. I moved
easily, the pack and the rifle seeming almost
weightless. I had a small hand axe looped into
my belt on one side, the Blacks' pistol secured
on the other.

I kept to the tops of the ridges as much as
possible, because the vegetation in the valleys
made for pretty slow going. It was hot, but not
unbearably so, and after about two hours, I hit
Mr. Castapolous's first landmark, a rocky hill
at the end of one of those plateaus that are so
common in the Ozarks. A quarter of a mile of
open grassland led to this strange formation,
about two stories high with overlapping ledges
giving it the look of a giant tiered wedding
cake. That's exactly what Mr. Castapolous had
told me to write down on the map: "wedding cake
hill."

As I stood looking at it and then the map, I
became aware of squirrels frisking about under
the trees to my right. What the heck, I
thought. Fresh meat, and I needed to practice a
little with the Mannlicher anyway. So I swung
it up, took a bead on the tree rat nearest me,

and squeezed off. I was prepared for the
recoil. What I wasn't prepared for was the
caliber of the gun. That squirrel exploded like
a cherry bomb. I switched to one that had
leaped to a tree trunk, this time aiming just
ahead of him. Another boom! echoed off the
facing of the hill and reverberated away, and I
saw the gaping hole I'd shot in the trunk, the
squirrel laid out underneath it. You remember
how we used to "bark" squirrels, hitting a spot
right next to them and knocking them out with
the concussion? That's what I did here, only
with a lot more powerful weapon than we ever
used.

It was loud, too, and since I didn't want to
give myself away, I decided to be satisfied
with one squirrel. I cleaned him on the spot —
as much to make sure he was dead as anything
else — and put him in a game sack, figuring he
ought to last until I could pop him in the pot
for supper.

I soldiered on for a few more hours, until I
got to the final landmark, a valley choked with
sumac, wild plums, honey locusts, persimmon
trees, and bois d'arc. It was a good place to
stop and slake the hunger I'd felt for hours,
made even better by the close proximity of a
creek where I could wash my hands.

As I chewed on my summer sausage, cheese,
and prospector's biscuits, with a couple of
handfuls of raisins thrown in, I studied the
valley. The brush was too dense for even a deer
to get in there. Maybe some of the wild hogs

Mr. Castapolous told me about, but nothing any bigger.

At the thought of hogs, I became a bit more wary. Scanning the valley's vegetation, I saw dead burnt trees sticking up out of the thicket, and I wondered what had burned them. Probably just wildfire, I thought, but then I got the unmistakable feeling that men had been responsible. In fact, for a few moments there I could almost see people running through the acres and acres of brush in front of me, shooting, screaming, tearing their clothes on the brush and trees. It was the seventh sense, I'm sure, honed to a fine edge because I was here in the wilderness, alone. And as those half-seen images skittered and faded through the brush, I began thinking about old Ezekiel Andras and the story he'd told me about the exploits of the post-Civil War renegades. With a shock, I <u>knew</u> that this was the very area Mr. Andras had described, the box canyon that had been set ablaze to burn the raiders out. Nearly seventy-five years later, those blackened sentinels in the thicket stood as mute testimony to the murderous event, and the ghosts that fluttered by me confirmed it. They were blackened, too.

John, I know this sounds like something right out of old William Hope Hodgson, but I figure if you've stayed with me this long, through all the inexplicable doings in Mackaville, you won't turn away in disbelief at this late date.

The ghosts soon faded, as did the feeling that I was in the midst of that long-ago deadly conflagration, and after a couple of minutes I was breathing normally again and hungry enough to finish the remnants of my lunch.

I'd been sitting on a big slab of rock, about the size of your folks' dining-room table. It was half in the sun and half in the shade. I was sitting on the shady side, of course, and when I reached over for my pack I saw movement out of the corner of my eye and froze. A big rattler, maybe six feet long, had crawled up onto the sunny side of the rock. His head slightly raised and swaying, he watched me, his tongue flicking in and out. There was no rattling, though, no warning that he was about to strike. I'd say he was no more than ten feet away from me, and that was a distance he could easily cover in a second or two if he changed his mind.

I stared at him, looking into those reptilian eyes, and as my hand slowly moved toward the pistol in my belt all I could think of was Old Man Black.

Before I could get my weapon out, that snake turned and dropped off the rock, slithering away. I stood up, gauging his passage by the swaying of the tall grass in the clearing as he headed toward the vegetation-choked valley. It took me a moment to realize I still had a Baker's chocolate bar in my mouth — which I can damn well tell you was dry as the Gobi — and the pack dangling from my right hand.

I allowed myself one shudder and then shouldered into the pack, settling it into place, picking up the rifle, and considering the implications of what I'd just seen. Maybe, I thought, there weren't any. Maybe it was just an old snake sunning himself.

But, hell, I knew better. Black's reach extended clear out here. Maybe he wanted me to know that. And maybe he also wanted me to know that our agreement was still in effect, so no snake attack.

This time.

Snakes — damn, I hate 'em.

About two hours later I dropped off another ridge into a valley with a creek running through it. I was sure had to be the last leg to my objective. Inexplicably then, I suddenly got an attack of the jitters. It was weird. Trying to pay as little attention to my shakes as possible, I took off my boots and leggings and started wading up the creek that followed the bottom between the ridges Mr. Castapolous had told me about. The water was warm, almost hot, and at one point it came up almost to my knees. Little minnows darted and swooped in schools around my ankles.

It took another half-mile before I spotted the wall, atop a long straight stretch of the valley on the side of the right ridge. I could see the stones Mr. Castapolous had seen, the evidence of a man-made shelter. And I realized I wasn't shivering anymore.

Stepping out of the water, I dried my feet,

pulled on my socks and boots and leggings, and climbed up the ridge — finding myself thinking again about that damned snake and Old Man Black.

Well, I'm sorry, but that's about all I can write this time. I'm beat as hell. After a night's worth of rest, I promise to tell you more. A lot more.

Your friend and faithful correspondent,
Robert

July 22, 1939
   late Friday night/early Saturday morning

Dear John,
   Looking back, I see I wrote that I "climbed
up the ridge." That was a story-telling
shortcut I took because I was too damn tired to
go into detail. Getting to the cave wasn't as
simple as that. The creek is surrounded by
smooth rock, rising up on both sides at a
seventy-five or eighty degree angle in most
places, and I had to backtrack about a hundred
yards before I could find a place that wasn't
too steep for me to climb. Once I got to the
top of the ridge I encountered a tangle of
trees, brush, and dead wood, which I knew from
my CCC days was a blow-down, a place where a
tornado or high winds had come through in the
past. It was too thick for me to go through,
and it was full of honey locusts — those trees
with mean thorns as long as your little finger
— so I had to go around it, which took some
time. That was ok though. Now I knew where I'd
be able to get all the firewood I needed.
   By the time I'd worked my way to the other
side of the blow-down, I could see in detail
Mr. Castapolous's wall, a kind of parapet that
hid the narrow trail leading to the opening of
the cave. A few steps more, and I was in front
of the cave's mouth, the remnants of a door
rotting around it. Once again, I had the

feeling that I was near to those long-dead raiders — very near.

Right then, I would've bet dollars to donuts that this very cave was their main hideout. It had a sort of aura about it, like old Fort Snelling, where all those Indian people died. Remember when we went there together? It didn't take a seventh, or even a sixth, sense to get the feeling that came from that place. You felt it just like I did.

So I stood there for a couple of minutes, soaking up the impressions I was getting, and then, squatting down, I peered inside. The way the wall was structured, there was no way to see the mouth of the cave from down below, and if the elements hadn't eroded away the clay over the years it would've been hard to tell that the wall was even there to begin with.

The sun was in the right spot for me to be able to see into a stone room that was a good twenty or thirty feet square. Mr. Castapolous had been right about the little spring, too, a thread of water trickling down the wall and into a small channel before it disappeared into a hole — a crack, really — in the cave floor.

It was a sweet spot to hide out in, a natural fort, and while Mr. Castapolous had prepared me for the fact that it had been inhabited, when I glimpsed the circle of fireplace stones back about ten feet from where I squatted it really came home to me that this had to be the place where those renegades of three generations past had hung their hats and plotted their dirty deeds.

Now that I'd found the place, the next order of business was to clear out any creepy-crawlies. I gathered up an armload of dry leaves and twigs that had collected inside the walkway and piled them in the fireplace. Then I went back to the blow-down and cut a red cedar about the size of a small Christmas tree, bringing it back and throwing it on the leaf pile. Finally, I gathered up some of the "fruit" off a bois d'arc tree — what the people around here call horse apples. You know what I'm talking about: green hard things about the size of a grapefruit. They're supposed to be good for keeping spiders and bugs away.

With the horse apples on top of the leaves and the cedar tree, I touched it all off with a match. The fire took hold pretty quickly, and I had to hop outside when that cedar flared up and flames and smoke licked around the entrance. There were more flames than smoke, though, and after about thirty minutes, when I was able to enter again, I saw that the smoke was being sucked up through a big crack in the granite ceiling of the cave. I didn't know where it came out, but I suspected it was some-where far up on the ridge. Just another reason this place was ideal for a hideout. If you burned hard wood, there would be almost no smoke, and what there was wouldn't give you away.

Over the past couple of hours, the excitement I'd felt when I'd discovered the cave had slowly dissolved into something else. Nerves, maybe, or my seventh sense again. I felt there had been something evil living in this place, and I was trespassing somewhere I didn't belong. The feeling came and went, but it seemed to be staying longer and longer each time.

I spent the next swath of my time gathering firewood as well as some stouter logs. Luckily, I didn't have to drag those too far, as I was able to find what I needed in that handy nearby blow-down. I also got the inspiration to cut several honey-locust branches that were full of those wicked thorns. Then, I pulled up several armloads of that tall mountain grass, which I took back to stuff into my browse bag in order to make a passable mattress. Once I was back at the cave, I spread the thorny branches across the path to the opening, removed the top layer of stones from the outside wall, propped the logs up in the opening, and stacked those stones behind them to hold everything in place. I might not be able to do anything about the ghosts inside, but I could damn sure keep anything outside from coming in — and if something did, I hoped the combination of the honey-locust thorns and the barricade of logs and stones would slow it down enough for me to draw a bead on it.

By the time I finished with everything it was beginning to get dark, so I built up a nice big fire, sat down against the barricade, and

started writing you that first missive,
listening to the water in the small pot begin
to boil merrily above the fire and around the
squirrel I'd shot. When I started craving a
break from getting this story down on paper, I
got up and began poking around the outer edges
of the interior, using Jolley's wind-up flashlight to look in places where the glow from the
fire didn't reach. It was that flash that
showed me a couple of potentially valuable
things. First, I saw that there was another
opening in the back of the cave. It was a lot
smaller, and it almost butted up against the
rock and dirt that towered into the sky above
it, but it was an exit, and it could possibly
come in handy.

Then, on a shelf close by, I found two
little kegs, sitting on a rock ledge way back
in a dark corner. I touched one and was
surprised to find it sticky. Taking it down
with both hands, I set it near the fire and saw
that it was coated with something that looked
and felt like tar — pine tar, maybe, or some
other kind of pitch.

There didn't seem to be any easy way to open
it, so I got out my axe and knocked the top in.
I was floored when I saw the contents. It was
full of brass powder horns, the bottle-shaped
kind with a short little brass pipe on top to
measure the charge for an old black-powder
weapon. It didn't take me long to realize that
I was looking at the ammunition supply for
whoever had last used the cave as a hideout —

which I felt even surer now were Mr. Ezekiel Andras's renegades from the Civil War days. They sure hadn't been hurting for ammo. I took the paper sack that Dill Jolley had put my prospector's biscuits and summer sausage in and shook out the powder horns into it. There were thirteen of them, and when I was finished, I had a sack full of black powder that weighed at least a couple of pounds. Even though it was very old, black powder doesn't deteriorate like regular gunpowder, so unless it had gotten wet or otherwise compromised — highly unlikely, given its storage conditions — I had little doubt it was potent and was careful to keep the bag well away from the fire.

Then, another surprise. When I got to the bottom of the keg I found a loaded Colt Walker .44 caliber, a huge old black-powder pistol, that had a bit of rust on it but otherwise in pretty good shape. My first thought was that now I'd found some relics that I could bring back and share with Mr. Castapolous, just as I'd told him I'd try to do. They might even be worth some money, and of course we'd share that, too. It felt fine to think that I'd be able to repay him for the loan of the Mannlicher as well as for his other kindnesses, including letting me in on the location of this place.

Packing the now-emptied horns in my pack, I cleaned the gun a little bit but decided I'd better not try to unload it until I got back home. There was just enough rust to complicate the process. So I carefully stashed it in my pack with the horns and turned my attention to the other keg.

It was also covered with pitch but a lot lighter, and when I got it down and hacked off its top, all I found inside was a small ledger book with surnames and amounts of money beside them. I recognized a lot of the names from Mackaville — Gabber, Black, McDermott, and Gibson, among others. I figured it was some sort of a record of how they'd divided the spoils of their raids, and it certainly warranted further study, so I stuck it in my pack, which was now getting pretty full. I'd pore over it once I got back to town.

By this time, I figured the squirrel had been parboiled enough to make him tender and kill most of the gamey taste, so I drained the boiling water into the little groove in the cave floor, got out the tin of bacon and fried it up with the squirrel, and then ate it all with the last of the hard cheese. Then, checking the barricade once more, I continued writing my earlier letter to you until I got too tired to go on anymore. I lay down on my stuffed browse bag and quickly found myself drifting off.

After a little over an hour, according to my strap watch, I awoke, alarm bells ringing crazily inside my head. The fire was still glowing at the ends of a few logs, so I could see a little, and at first nothing looked wrong or out of place. As I lay there, facing the cave's entrance, I focused on a couple of stars I spied through the crack in the top of my barricade. Then it hit me — I shouldn't be able to see those stars. I'd left a small gap in the rocks and logs so I could see directly outside. Somehow, the hole had shifted to a different angle.

At the same time, I heard an unmistakable creaking noise at the mouth of the cave. There had to be at least a couple hundred pounds of logs and rocks piled up there, and as I watched, it started to bow inward, pushing toward me, something huge and powerful shoving from behind it.

My Colt Cavalry .45, the gift from Seth Black, was under the wadded-up raincoat I had for a pillow, and I jerked it up and fired in one motion. The sudden noise of that first shot echoed maniacally through the cave, but I hardly noticed. I did notice I'd been fairly accurate, blowing a chunk out of the top log just under the gap before the bullet spanged out into the night.

Leaping up, I ran to the barricade and kept firing out through the crack, moving the barrel back and forth. The ledge in front was narrow, so I figured my chances were good to hit anything that happened to be out there. I emptied the pistol, started reloading.

As I shoved bullets in their chambers, I tried to listen through the ringing in my ears. Once the reverberations from the pistol had faded, it had become quiet as a tomb out there

— no frogs, no crickets, no night birds. Nothing. And, although my hearing hadn't quite recovered, I distinctly picked up the sound of something blundering into that blow-down tangle of dead wood and brush on the ridge, followed by an awful howling. I'd been able to avoid the honey locusts and their thorns while I was pulling logs and firewood out of there; whatever this was hadn't been as lucky.

The howling stopped after a while, and the woods outside the cave died into silence again. I restacked the logs and stone, built up the fire, and propped myself against a far wall of the cave, the Mannlicher rifle across my legs. That's how I spent the rest of the night, too keyed-up to sleep. Finally, I picked up pencil and paper and started writing these lines to you, while I waited for a second siege that never came.

Not exactly how I'd planned to relax in the mountains, but as that Harvard prof from Austria — Shumpter? — said a while back, we always plan too much and think too little.

The first rays of sunlight will be coming over the ridgebacks soon. I'll go outside then and see what I can find. I started to write "wish me luck," but by the time you get this you'll know full well whether I had any luck or not.

Your tired but faithful correspondent,
Robert

July 24, 1939
Monday morning
Saint Louis, Missouri

Dear John,

Yes, I _do_ have quite a bit of explaining to do.

I know you're wondering about a lot of things, like why I mailed you two days' worth of handwritten journal entries and then went silent for a couple days, or why I'm once again using a typewriter or, hell, why in the world I'm writing you from St. Louis, Missouri. (I know you glimmed the postmark.) I hope you got the long-distance message I left at the _Dispatch_ newsroom yesterday, that I was ok and you'd be hearing from me soon; the switchboard operator told me you weren't there but she'd make sure you got it.

I think back now, remembering how I sat propped up against the wall of that cave, stoking the fire occasionally to give me enough light to write you, trying to focus my thoughts on the page instead of whatever was outside and had tried to get in. It was only last Saturday, but it seems like a million years ago.

I didn't know what was out there, but whatever it was had been plenty strong enough to move a couple hundred pounds of logs and stone. So I waited until daylight, carefully opened up a side of the barricade and squeezed through, the Mannlicher clutched in my hands.

The first shock I got was the sight of a man's footprint, big and bare, in the dust outside the entrance. It raised the hair on my arms and the back of my neck, and all I could think was that it wasn't bad enough to have snakes after me — now some barefoot son-of-a-bitch was trying to get me, too. For a few seconds, I wondered if it was the Blacks, but I quickly discarded the notion. While I wouldn't put it past them to sniff me out in these hills, they would've said something before trying to bust their way in. Plus, despite their hill-billy ways, I'd never seen either of them, or their old man, go shoeless.

I stood there and thought for a minute, then an idea hit me. Always making sure to keep an eye out for any movement outside, I went back in and loaded up my stuff. Then I checked that rear exit a little more closely. Sure enough, there wasn't much room between the opening and the side of the cliff that rose above it, but in the daylight I could see some rock outcroppings and, maybe, a few man-made handholds.

Satisfied, I started a good fire up again. I didn't plan on cooking breakfast, though — a few swallows of spring water and a chunk of chocolate made do for that. Instead, working as fast as I could, I gathered up some of the flattest rocks I could find and put together a small fire reflector. You remember what that is: a little structure that's supposed to help throw the heat from a fire into your lean-to or tent. We tried it a couple of times in our younger days. What it really does is act as a wind block so the embers of the fires don't blow around. I had my reasons for choosing a place for the reflector close to the fireplace, directly between it and the cave opening.

Once it was finished, I rolled a big rock between it and the fire and balanced the paper bag full of black powder on top of it, close, but not too close, to the fire, and tilted just slightly toward it. Then I secured a piece of twine around the top of the bag and, taking both ends, ran them about six inches off the cave floor and tied them around rocks on either side of the room.

What I hoped was that anyone entering would trip the twine and throw the bag into the fireplace, with most unpleasant results. Because of the fire reflector, I reasoned that whoever it was wouldn't see any embers swirling around and probably wouldn't glimpse the bag right away. I wasn't positive the booby-trap would work — the powder could land away from the flames, for instance — but it was well worth a try. I wanted not only to know who or what was following me, but also to at least slow whatever it was down.

After replacing the parts of the barricade I'd moved, leaving that crack at the top, I shaped my browse bag into a reasonable-looking facsimile of a person, draped my blanket over the lower half of it, and placed it against the back wall, as though I had fallen asleep with my face turned away from the entrance. Then I peed all around it. I'd already taken a couple of leaks into that groove in the floor, so the place had a slight "perfume." I wanted it strong enough that my attacker would think I was still in there, rush the dummy, and trip the cord that threw the powder into the fire.

That was the plan, anyway.

I filled my canteen at the spring, then took up my load and pushed it all out the back door of the cave, along with the Mannlicher, which I slung around my back after I exited. Then I began to climb. It wasn't easy by any means, and a couple of times I almost took a tumble, but by the time the sun was over the hills north of me I'd finally reached the top of the cliff and sat for a moment, looking at the creek that now lay six or seven hundred feet straight down. I planned on doubling back by another route, finding my bike, and getting the hell out of that place.

I was still gazing at the scenery below and catching my breath when I heard a powerful WHOMP! from below. The cliff had rounded out so I couldn't see the cave entrance from where I sat, but a big blast of black smoke pushed out over the creek below me and, I swear, a couple of things that looked like big dogs shot through it, wailing like banshees as they plunged to the creek bed below.

My trap had worked, although I didn't know how well. If anything had survived the blast, I was sure it would be after me with a vengeance.

Survived, I thought. Was I now a murderer?

I hadn't considered that when I'd planned and constructed my trap. I'd just been worried about saving my own ass. But as I picked up and jogged off, the idea preyed on my mind. Among other things, I'd come out here in the mountainous wilds to confront myself, to see if I was really capable of killing a person, even a person as odious as Old Man Black. Now, almost offhandedly, I may have murdered someone, or several someones, in absolute cold blood. Those were undoubtedly animals I'd just seen flying through the air, but no beast had left that human footprint outside the cave.

I'd gone maybe five miles in what my compass told me was the right direction, the images of mangled smoking bodies twisting through my mind despite my best efforts to think about something else — like how winded I was — when I came to that wedding-cake hill that had been my first landmark on the trip. There was a little knob of ground behind it that rose almost to the first rocky tier. Summoning up what little strength I had left, I managed to clamber up it and onto that bottom ledge, where I shrugged off my pack and rolled over on my back, gazing up at the sky and gasping for breath. I knew I had to get a little rest before I pushed on, and even though I didn't know how close my pursuers were, or if I had any at all, I felt as though this were as safe a place as any. If someone were on my trail, I ought to be able to see them from here.

After my breathing returned to normal, I got

to my knees, took a good drink from the canteen, and broke off another chunk of Baker's chocolate. I was chewing on that when I spied some movement down at the end of the meadow in the trees, a good five hundred yards away.

At first, I couldn't make out what it was, just vague impressions. Then, at the edge of the meadow, some of the greenery began moving, and I knew that whatever it might be was heading in my direction. So I picked up the Mannlicher carbine, made sure the magazine was filled with those big shells, and put a dozen more in a handkerchief I laid down beside me. Whatever it turned out to be, I was going to be ready.

Then all at once a big sounder of feral hogs burst into the meadow, snuffling and squealing and — I swear — headed for me. I knew this as surely as I knew anything. They were a single unit with one goal in mind: to see me dead.

It all came to me in a flash — I was going to have to fight for my life. I supposed it was the seventh sense, and if it was, it has never been clearer. Oddly, mixed in with this realization were fleeting images of the Gabbers and that vicious hog vs. snake donnybrook I'd witnessed at their farm.

Steadying the Mannlicher on the rock edifice in front of me, I flipped the rear sight up and adjusted for range, removing the pistol from my belt at the same time and setting it beside me. Then, pulling my cap down tight and low over my forehead, I drew a bead on the lead hog and squeezed off a round. He flipped like a marlin, shooting up in the air and twisting before he crashed to the ground.

It was a grisly sight, but it didn't stop those damn pigs for a second. If I'd had any doubts at all, I knew then for sure that they weren't ordinary hogs, feral or otherwise, because regular ones would've scattered like quail after that first shot. Instead, these kept coming in a fast trot, quickly narrowing the yards between them and me, blood in their eyes. I snapped my next shot at a big black one, thinking it looked just like one of the surly hogs at the Gabber place, and down he went.

I didn't need the sight now — they were too close — so I flipped it down and kept right on shooting. Six shots, six pigs hit. Grabbing up a handful of shells from the handkerchief beside me, I reloaded in record time, and that was good because they were closing in fast.

Six more went down, and I silently thanked God for Mr. Castapolous and his gift of this beautiful precision weapon. Then I was out of ammunition again, even as a pair of hogs closed to within a few dozen yards of me. I got two rounds in the Mannlicher and then dropped a shell. I didn't have time to pick it up. The beasts were almost directly in front of me, so close I could see the strings of saliva slinging out of their ugly mouths.

Slapping the bolt home, I blasted one of them squarely between the eyes, but the other

one swerved as I fired a second shot, missing
cleanly.

It disappeared then and for a moment, with
the sounds of all the shots echoing wildly
around my brain, I couldn't hear it. Then I
heard a skittering behind me and realized it
was climbing up the same knob of earth I'd used
to gain access to the ledge. Turning, I scrambled to my feet, revolver in hand, just as that
big mad hog came tearing around the ledge
toward me. I fired two shots into him and then
he was on me, slashing at my legs with his
tusks. The only thing I could do was jump.

On this side, the ledge was a good ten feet
above ground level, and the best I could hope
for was that the hog, maddened as he seemed to
be, would dive down after me and break a leg. I
thought of this just as I hit the grassy earth
myself and went rolling, still holding the
pistol to my chest in a death grip.

The hog was smarter than I'd figured. He
snorted and looked down at me for a moment, and
then raced around to the back of the tier,
where he could scramble down the knob of
ground.

Then I got a jolt. As I started pulling
myself to my feet a hard tug on my left sleeve
threw me back down with a ripping sound and I
found myself staring into the enraged red eyes
of a not-dead-enough wild pig. I didn't realize
I'd pulled the trigger on the pistol until his
brains exploded in front of my face, showering
me with gore. I staggered up just in time to

face the animal from the ridge, charging at me from around the corner of wedding-cake hill. Steadying as much as you can in that sort of situation, I let a .45 slug fly. It probably flattened on his skull, but it was enough to blow bone splinters into his brain, and he abruptly skidded on his nose, blood flying from his nostrils. Two more shots through the top of his head and I was running for my life around to that knob and back onto the ledge, where I dropped the pistol and began jamming shells into the Mannlicher.

I'd spotted two more huge black boars still standing in the midst of the carnage. Once again, I was reminded of those intimidating, detached hogs at the Gabber's, standing back from the action as though they were directing it. These gave me exactly the same feeling. And at the same time, it came to me: the Gabbers had to be involved, somehow, in this. It was a thought I couldn't mull over because of the necessity of direct action, but I knew it was right.

Despite shaking as though I'd come down with a sudden case of Saint Vitus Dance, I managed to get those big shells loaded in the Mannlicher. I may have been close to going into shock, but by damn I was determined to fight to the last breath.

Then I stood up, Mannlicher in hand — and they were gone. Just gone. Dead and dying hogs all around, multicolored carnage, agonized death rattles twisting through the air, but no sign of those two. I watched and waited and watched some more, until my case of the trembles subsided. Then I picked up my pistol, reloaded it, and stuck it back in my belt. Shrugging into my pack, I pulled myself together and got the hell out of there, thinking that with all the climbing and hiking and shaking I'd been doing I'd probably already lost about five pounds.

Just reliving all that has worn me out. I'll write more in an hour or two and won't mail this until I have everything down for you, but right now I just have to lie down for a little while. So I'll sign off, but not for long. Lots more coming, you bet.

Your pal and faithful correspondent,
Robert

July 24, 1939
(continued)

Dear John,

I really hope I have the poop to give you all of this, an enormous amount of information that I think it's very important for you to have. I don't know how long I've got to put it all down, either, before I have to go on the move again, so I'll do all I can at this sitting. I don't plan to leave this boarding-house room until I get you up to date, but you know about what can happen to "plans."

And now, we return to Robert, the hogs, and the everlasting hills of Arkansas...

The Mannlicher again strapped across my back, I ran in a straight line toward the place where I'd hidden my bike, leaping over the carcasses of dead and dying hogs and always keeping an eye out for those two black boars that had survived the massacre. Whatever was after me knew where I was. That fact was clear from the hog attack. I couldn't duck my pursuers, if there were any left — and I was sure there were. I could only hope they weren't of sufficient number to overwhelm me and, if they were, that they might have some trepidation after hearing the gunfire and coming onto the carnage that littered the landscape around wedding-cake hill.

And in all of this, I kept getting images of the Gabbers, which confused me. Weren't they my

friends? Hadn't they defended me against the
snakes? Why would they want to kill me? It was
crazy — although my life in the past few months
has given an expanded meaning to that word —
but I kept seeing that footprint outside the
cave opening and thinking, somehow, "Gabbers."

The straight line to my escape, unfortunately, ran up and down. So I plunged into the
woods and through them down into the valley
that lay between me and the big Indian. The
woods thinned out a little as I hit the
valley's bottom and immediately encountered
several sink holes, which told me that the
ground there was undercut by caves. These holes
looked like giant doodlebug pits. I'd run onto
them before out in these mountains, on some of
my interview trips, and I'd studied them enough
to know that they were the result of caves that
got washed out of the limestone and lay under a
thin layer of granite or some other hard rock.
If one of those caves expands enough, the rock
roof collapses and you have a sink hole.

Some of the ones surrounding me now were
very impressive, maybe a half-block across, and
I slowed down so I could steer my way through
them. I'd been through too damn much to die in
a fall through a sink hole because of my own
carelessness.

I was about halfway across the bottom of the
valley when I heard the unmistakable sound of
something big crashing through some brush up
the slope behind me. That's when I got stupid
and looked back, taking my eyes off the path.

The next instant I was in midair, kicking at nothing, and then, WHAM!, I landed on my back against the side of one of those holes and began skidding downward toward the opening in the roof of the cave. There was no way of knowing how far it was to the cave's bottom — maybe hundreds of feet, I thought with a shock, even as I tried to scrabble up the dirt and rock that cascaded around me. Silently asking Mr. Castapolous's forgiveness, I pulled the Mannlicher around and managed to jab its butt into the side of the sink hole, underneath the sliding earth. Remarkably, it held. I hung on, dirt clods pinging against the walls of the cave beneath me, and my feet found a thin rocky lip around that big hole in the cave's roof. I'd no more than put all my weight on it when I heard a distinct cracking sound. That's when I knew I'd have to try and crawl back up the side. The lip could give way at any moment.

Then things got worse.

As I hung onto the rifle, panting, trying not to put all my weight on the thin rock ledge under my feet, I heard a grunting noise from the top of the sink hole, which was maybe twenty feet up. Suddenly, the wild-animal faces of those two huge black boars jutted into the hole, blotting out most of the daylight behind them. And for all their bristles and tusks and wild eyes, they looked somehow human.

The name, once again, came to me unbidden: Gabber.

In addition to looking human, they also

looked like they knew they had me where they wanted me. I didn't trust my foothold enough to pull the rifle butt out of where it was anchored and take a shot at them, and a slap at my belt told me that my holster had worked around to the middle of my back, and the .45 revolver had slipped out. I saw that it had fallen near my feet, and I couldn't reach it.

The hogs grunted as though they were amused, looking at one another and then down at me, sticking their godforsaken snouts down into the hole, their piggy eyes regarding me. And then, I swear, John, they began to change.

I can't tell you exactly what it was — maybe it was smoke or mist or something obscuring their faces, but then maybe their features just kind of melted. Whatever happened, I was suddenly looking into the eyes of two men, an unspeakably dirty white guy with shoulder-length matted hair and a huge colored man who, if nothing else, was cleaner than his companion. Judging from what I could see, neither had on a stitch of clothing.

We stared at one another for what seemed like eons, and then the face of the white one disappeared from the hole. The black continued looking at me, saying nothing. Then I heard weird scratching and grinding sounds, seeming to come from the very depths of his soul, and he began opening and closing and moving his mouth around, as though he were testing and exercising muscles he hadn't used in a very long time. Noises close to speech grated from his throat. He seemed to be trying to communicate with me.

Before that could happen, his partner returned. Just as I glimpsed a big log, wielded like a club, in one of the white's grimy hands, he babbled a kind of laugh and then stuck his filthy naked ass into the hole and gained a foothold on one side.

The bastard was climbing down after me!

I saw he might be able to do it, too. The small landslide I'd caused had subsided, exposing some thick tree roots and rock outcroppings. If only they hadn't been up there, I could've climbed to freedom now. Instead, it was just the opposite. My way was blocked by a slowly descending unclothed savage who intended to knock me down into the cave or simply bash my brains out.

Fighting back panic, I tried to figure my way out of this spot. I couldn't pull the Mannlicher out of the side of the sink hole, because the rim above the cave might not hold my full weight. My pistol lay somewhere around my feet, beyond my grasp.

And then I remembered the ancient Colt Walker .44 in my pack, the one I'd gotten out of the cave. Keeping an eye on the grunting pig man who had now cut the distance between us in half, I managed to get one hand inside my pack and wrap it around the butt of the revolver. Then, very slowly, I pulled it out, cocked it, aimed squarely at him, and pulled the trigger.

There was a little "snap." Nothing more. He

had jerked back a little, wary, when I'd leveled the gun at him, but now he grinned evilly, teeth like boar tusks, and continued his advance toward me.

The gun, the powder, the caps, all nearly seventy-five years old. What could I have expected?

Still, I had no other hope. So I cocked it again and squeezed the trigger — and damned if a huge blast of acrid black smoke and flame didn't explode from the barrel, throwing the guy back against the side of the sink hole. When the smoke cleared I saw a big bloody place in his stomach. He dropped the club and stared dumbly at me, hanging onto a tree root with one hand, making a gabbling noise that sounded like nothing human. I cocked and fired, cocked and fired again, and he came somersaulting by in a rush of earth and rock, almost dislodging the Mannlicher as he slid past me and through that big opening under my feet, crumbling away a piece of the rock rim I stood on. He didn't scream, but after a few seconds I heard a sodden crash, flesh against rock at the cave's bottom, and I knew he was through.

I turned my attention then to his comrade. Counting the initial misfire, I figured I had two bullets left, with no guarantee that either would discharge. Still, I didn't have too many other options.

The ebony face peered in at me, eyes white, through the smoke and dust. He was muttering something that didn't sound like any language I knew, and he seemed to be having a frenzied conversation with himself, grunts and squeals and then, slowly, the introduction of some English words, as though he were remembering them from a very long time ago. He muttered more, never taking his eyes off me, and I heard something that sounded like "rocks" and then "roll" and "cave" and "kill." I may not have known exactly what he meant, but the implication was clear enough. He was going to start rolling rocks down the hole until he dislodged me and sent me falling into the cave.

I had my finger on the Colt Walker's hammer, raising it slowly to take the best shot I could, when he suddenly wailed, "FOR THE LOVE OF GOD — DAMN! HELP ME!" His eyes, locked into mine, were wild, the tortured voice barely recognizable as human, like the sound of a rasp on a lock. Then he screamed it again without the "damn," the same words, the same agonized intonation. He would've sounded like a preacher at a Baptist revival if the delivery hadn't reminded me of the squeal of brakes locking up and the grinding of metal on metal.

"All right," I said, loudly but as calmly as I could. "I will. But you have to help me, too. You have to help me get out of here." I still had one arm in a death grip around that anchored Mannlicher, trying not to put too much weight on the shaky rim that the pig man had partially destroyed. His slide had exposed a thick layer of shale maybe four feet above my head that might hold long enough for me to move up and grab one of the tree roots sticking out above it, and I thought from there I'd have enough handholds to make it to the top and out — if I was able to convince that colored man I really could help him. He didn't really have any reason to trust me, especially since I'd shot his companion.

He grunted. "Not much time," he said. "Throw me gun."

"I can't," I told him. "It'd put me off balance and I might fall in with your friend. How about if I stick it back in my pack?"

"All right." He grunted again. "Hurry."

I didn't need him to tell me that. As I got ready to ascend, I remembered the pistol at my feet, so I carefully felt around for it with my free hand and got lucky. I stuck it back in my belt and then, with the same hand, reached up and grabbed the side of the shale outcropping. It sloughed off a little but held, and I was able to pull the Mannlicher out, wrap its strap around me with the one hand, and start climbing. That big tree root protruded above and just to the right of the rock; I grabbed at it and was looking for the next handhold when the end of a big tree branch came bobbing toward me from the hole.

"Grab this," said the man. "I'll pull."

"Pull" wasn't quite the word for what happened when I wrapped both my hands around it and squeezed it to my body. He jerked me out so hard and fast that I damn near went airborne as I cleared the lip of the crater.

Rolling onto my back, I looked up into his eyes.

"You say... you could help me," he said. "Are you a conjure man?" His voice was a raspy near-whisper.

John, do you remember in a much earlier letter when I told you about first meeting the Gabber boys and how it was like God gave me the words to say when they caught me at their still? That feeling we've both had a few times in our lives?

This was one of those rare occasions.

Maybe part of it wasn't even supernatural, or seventh sense, or anything else like that. Maybe it was just knowing, from the evidence of my own eyes, that the naked man in front of me had not too much earlier been a wild hog, and that he likely wanted to stay human now.

"Yes," I said. "I'm a conjure man — and I can break the spell you're under."

His eyes widened. "Then, for the love of God — do it!" He shouted and grabbed my forearm almost hard enough to crack the bone. "I don't know how long I can hold this shape! And how long before they start seeing through my eyes again!"

I didn't know what he meant by either statement. What I did know was that I was in deep with no real idea how to deliver, but as you and I both know, magic works best when the people involved believe it's working. A verse from the Bible came to me then, something the father of the boy with an "evil spirit" said to

Christ: <u>Lord, I believe; help thou mine unbelief</u>.

And I got to work.

"Are you a Christian?" I snapped out. "What's your name? How old are you?"

"Hell, yes I'm a Christian," he returned, agitated. "I'm a preacher, African Methodist Episcopal. Even had a church in Mackaville once, for all the damn good it did me.

"My name is David Jefferson. I am — I <u>was</u> — forty-two years old. You need to hurry, mister."

At the same time he uttered that last sentence, the ground under us began to slide. He leapt forward, grabbing me around the waist, and we bounded ahead of the hole that had suddenly opened wider under our feet. We must've covered 100 yards, zig-zagging around a couple of other sink holes, before we stopped on a solid flat bed of granite. As he stood me up, I realized he'd handled me as though I weighed no more than a sheet of onionskin paper.

I don't know what I was going on — seventh sense, instinct, heavenly guidance, remembering stuff from my magic books. It didn't matter, because suddenly it was clear what I needed to do.

"Get me some kindling, David," I said. "Bark, grass, small twigs, anything. I'll help."

We started scavenging around the side of the valley nearest us, and I heard him come to a dead stop when I pulled my knife out of my leggings. Turning to him, I saw uncertainty in his eyes.

"Just wanted to cut a few green branches," I said. "I'll put it up after that."

He nodded and went back to his task.

Soon, we had a little stack of flammable material piled on the granite. Shrugging out of my pack and laying it and my rifle behind me, I got the fire going good and then quickly constructed a little stick man. For his part, David Jefferson stood stock still, looking back over his shoulder from time to time as though he expected something to be catching up with him. It was a silent plea for me to hurry.

Pulling the largest smoldering stick from the fire, I used the charcoal tip to draw a cross on the rock surface at our feet.

"Come here, Mr. Jefferson," I said. "Step beside me, but don't step on the cross."

I saw indecision flicker across his face, but he did as I said. Then, bending down, I drew a big circle around us.

"This will prevent them from knowing what we're doing," I said, wondering how I knew that, figuring I was going on pure instinct. Help thou mine unbelief.

"I — I still cannot feel them in my head, my eyes," he said, and for just a moment he almost smiled. "Praise Jesus. But keep working. Please."

I can only hope I looked more confident than I felt. Reaching down, I pulled a bandana and

tin cup out of my pack. Stretching out past the
confines of the circle, I skimmed the cup over
the rocks until I had it about half full of
earth.

"All right, Mr. Jefferson," I said, drawing
my knife. "Stick your arm out and hold still.
I'm going to need a little of your blood."

Hate to leave you cliff-hanging, John, but
once again I find myself so tired I can hardly
hit the keys. I'll catch a few winks and be
back soon with the rest of this story, I
promise.

Your pal and faithful correspondent,
Robert

July 24, 1939
    (<u>still</u> continued)

Dear John,

It's now a little after five o'clock on the north side of St. Louis, my current address. I feel really fagged, and I thought it'd help to lie down for a little bit and maybe nod off before giving you the rest of the tale of my first encounter with David Jefferson, but I can't seem to stay put. Just restless, I guess. Nervous energy. So I got up and stood outside the boarding house for a little bit, watching the workers roll back in from their jobs. They're mostly all colored men — with several women mixed in — getting off buses with their lunch buckets in their hands, heading off to homes and apartments and rooms not unlike this one.

But that's a different story for a different time. I'll give it to you later, but I can't get derailed now, not until I have all this down.

I just thought of something that gave me a bit of a chill: All of this has happened in less than a week since I headed into the Ozark mountains. Good Lord! Has it been just three days?

Damn! I'm getting ahead of myself again, and there's so much left to tell.

On with the story:

"Keep working," David Jefferson had told me.
And he'd talked about how he still couldn't
feel them in his mind and his eyes, which indicated to me that the magic was working so far,
or he thought it was working, which is, as I
think I wrote earlier, a lot the same thing.

In turn, I'd told him this ceremony would
keep "them" from knowing what we were doing.
But hell, I didn't really know what we were
doing either. I was going on pure instinct,
standing in this charcoal circle in the middle
of the Ozark mountains with a naked black man,
acting like I was some sort of wizard who saw
all and knew all.

Then again, on some level, I wasn't acting.
I sure as hell didn't know everything that was
going on — for starters, why everything was so
urgent and whom he'd meant by "they." But when
I'd scraped up a handful of dirt from around
the granite outcropping, it seemed as though my
hands were working under the influence of something deeper than my conscious mind, which at
the time was writhing with all sorts of half-
formed thoughts and images. It was like something was trying to break through and pull all
the chaos together into some cohesive, connect-
the-dots line. I kept getting visions of the
Gabbers, all mixed in with the ancient spells
I'd studied in my magic books, and bible verses
I'd learned in Sunday school at First Pres-
byterian in Hallock.

Try as I might, I couldn't get it all to

come together. Yet, somehow, the words were there when I needed them. Seventh sense, intuition, memory, divine guidance? All of it? I can't tell you. All I can say is that I somehow knew what to do. Or, hell, I hoped I did, anyway.

I turned to David Jefferson, who, watching me carefully, had extended his muscled right arm, holding his bicep with his right hand. When I stuck the point of my skinning knife into his forearm, going fairly deep but making sure not to hit a vein, he hardly flinched. Then, as the blood began trickling down his arm, I let it mix with the dirt in my cup until I had the right consistency. With my other hand, I pulled out the bandana.

"Here," I said, "tie this around it."

While he was wrapping the cloth around his forearm, I took up the little stick figure I'd made and packed the bloody mud around it, until it took on the rough contours of a human. Then I looked up at David Jefferson.

"This part is tricky, so listen carefully," I said, licking my suddenly dry lips. "I am going to place your soul in this little man—"

He gasped, stopping me, and I understood immediately that his soul was something of utmost importance to him, nothing to be fooled with. I held up a hand.

"Only for a few seconds. It's the ritual."

Before he could speak, I laid the figure atop the small fire and let it bake for about half a minute, watching the sweep hand of my strap watch. Then I took the charcoal-tipped stick and carefully raked it out to the center of the cross, where it lay smoldering. David watched apprehensively, his eyes darting back and forth between me and the figure.

"David," I said. "Do you have a middle name?"

He swallowed. "Yes. Garland. David Garland Jefferson." His speech was becoming almost normal.

I nodded and then turned my face to the sky, squinting against the afternoon sunlight.

"Our Father who lives in heaven and judges both the quick and the dead," I began. "I ask your help in removing the curse from your child, David Garland Jefferson, who has been washed in the blood of the Lamb and saved from perishing by your amazing grace. He trusts in you, Father, believing in the Father and the Son and the Holy Ghost. I ask now that his soul be migrated to the figure at our feet, only for such time as it takes to preserve him from the forces of evil."

I dropped down on my haunches and began remodeling the blood and dirt from a rough approximation of a human into the figure of a pig. The fire had rendered it less malleable, but I did the best I could, shaping what had been arms and legs into four porcine feet and flattening the face, pulling out the nose and ears. When I held it up, David Jefferson's gasp told me it was good enough for him.

Standing back up, I squeezed the little

effigy in my right hand, raised it into the air, and addressed the big sky again.

"With your help, Almighty Father, I now burn away the curse on David Jefferson and send it back to the evil one that put it on him!" And I tossed the thing into the fire.

Was I flying blind? Hell, yes. But the words, the gestures, came and it was as though I was just hanging on for the ride. Images burst and transformed and died all around me — people sitting in church, the stone tablets of the Ten Commandments, worn and leather-covered bibles, magic symbols, wizards in peaked hats, voodoo dolls, and, most surprisingly, the faces of the two Gabbers, distorted with rage. In the midst of all this tumult, I heard myself shout: "The Lord's Prayer, Mr. Jefferson! Say it!"

He launched right into it in a beautifully rich and rolling old-time-preacher's voice that carried none of the hesitation and rustiness of a few minutes earlier. And as he recited those time-honored words, coming down hard in all the right places, I shouted at the sky: "In the name of God Almighty! _Free_ this man's soul! Keep praying, David Jefferson!"

He did, the orison coming fast and hot from his lips.

"In the name of all that's pure and noble and right and holy," I intoned, "I send David Jefferson's soul back into himself, to safety and security under the breastplate of faith!" And John, damned if the little fire didn't flare up around what was left of my effigy,

shooting sparks around our ankles — and, dammit
John, it made a <u>noise</u>, a squealing noise like a
punctured tire!

Sure, a sudden wind could've accounted for
all of it, or a branch exploding from the heat.
But for whatever reason, when I looked down the
figure was gone. Vanished without so much as a
trace of ash. Dissipated into the summer's air.

David Jefferson was watching, even as he
prayed the Lord's Prayer for what must've been
a second or third time, slowing as he reached
"the <u>kingdom</u> and the <u>power</u> and the <u>glo-ry</u>
forever." Then, with a fervent, "Amen," he
turned to me and tears began gently rolling
down his face.

"I'm free," he whispered. "Finally at last.
I'm free." Before I knew it, he had his naked
arms around me in a bear hug and was kissing
me, first on one cheek and then the other.
Stepping back, he said, "Thank you. You do not
know."

"No," I said, "but maybe you'll tell me."

He nodded. "It has... it's been so long
since I was a man. They must've let that happen
so we could climb down the sinkhole and do you
in. They've been watching you for a long time.
They watched you through me. I don't know what
is going to happen now."

I thought about being trapped in that place
with those two wild animals grunting down at
me, changing form and shape and becoming human
— after a fashion. It seemed a lifetime ago.

"I am...a man," he said slowly, and then

looked down at his unclothed body, the sun, just beginning to lower behind the peak of the highest mountain around us, making a kind of aura behind him. Maybe it was the religious images that had been pinwheeling through my mind, but I couldn't help but think of the part in Genesis where Adam and Eve first realize they're naked.

"We can step out of the circle now," I said. "And hang on just a minute."

My pack was a few paces away, propped up against a big rock, and I dug into it and came up with a pair of boxer shorts and that Abercrombie & Fitch rain jacket. "Here," I said. "Hope they'll do until we can get you properly outfitted."

They did, but barely. His frame was so big that the jacket bulged at the shoulders and biceps. Still, he seemed grateful, stretching out his arms and shaking them under the sleeves.

"I'm a man," he said again. "I don't feel them anymore."

"Them?" I asked.

He rolled his eyes toward the heavens. "Praise God!" he intoned loudly. "I'm free!" Then he turned to me, his features tightening. "But they're near," he said. "They know you're here, and they want you dead. Me, too, I think."

"Then we'd better get on the road," I said. "But first, one last touch, Jefferson."

"Please call me David."

I grinned. "You bet," I said, sticking out my hand. It almost disappeared in his big black mitt. "I'm Robert. Robert Brown. Used to be CCC, so I picked up the habit of calling guys by their last names."

He looked at me blankly. "CCC?"

"Yeah. You know — Civilian Conservation Corps. FDR's WPA."

A smile split his face then, and he shook his head. "Lots of letters...Robert."

That's when I realized he had no earthly idea what I was talking about.

I freed my hand from his and fished around in my pants pocket, latching onto that big silver dollar I've always carried for luck. If I needed anything right then it was luck, but whatever had been guiding me during that whole ceremony was now telling me to give David Jefferson something tangible, to seal his transformation for good in his eyes. I can't exactly tell you why I drew out that silver piece and scratched a crude cross over the eagle with the tip of my knife. Once again, I just knew it was the right thing to do.

"Put this in the pocket of your jacket, David," I said. When he looked puzzled, I added, "Until you can get your hands on a real crucifix or a bible, this'll keep you safe. And be sure to snap that pocket shut."

Then, I was moved to do something I still don't understand. I pulled the Colt Cavalry revolver out of my belt and handed it to him, then reached in my front pocket and handed him all the rounds I had. His eyes lit up as he took it from me and turned it over in his hands, checking to see if it was loaded, and stuffing the bullets I'd given him in his pocket.

"I have lost track of all time, but I know I haven't held one of these since, I believe, the year 1877." He blew the dirt off it, wiped its stock with the rain jacket, sighted down its barrel. "We used to have to shoot targets at a gallop," he said. "I was pretty fair at it."

Mentally, I was busy trying to figure. If he'd been old enough to shoot a pistol in 1877 — why, hell, that was more than 50 years ago! And this big Negro man didn't look a day over 30.

Hefting the pistol, he said offhandedly, "You've kept it nice. Used it to kill those two pigs down at that big layered rock, didn't you?"

I guess my mouth dropped open a little then, because he went on quickly, "Don't worry. It was good and fast shooting, and they weren't friends of mine. None of them are."

Abruptly, he raised his head, looking back to the south of us.

"They're close," he said. "They're trying to take me over again. I feel them in my brain." He closed his eyes hard, fumbling open his pocket and grabbing the silver dollar I'd just given him. Clutching it in one of his ham fists, he stood stock still, while a horrible thought skittered through me: What if all that business I'd just done was just fairy dust? What if it hadn't worked at all, and David Garland Jefferson was about to become a feral hog again? I couldn't rely on the cap and ball pistol, and there was a good chance the Mannlicher was inoperative, too, thanks to what it had been through in the sinkhole.

And then, a bigger question: I knew him as a man now. No matter what he became, could I kill him?

All these thoughts flashed through me as I stared at David Jefferson, standing still as a statue. Once, John, I swear I saw his flesh ripple. Then, after what seemed like hours, he said, without opening his eyes or moving another muscle on his body, "There are four of them. Two big Russian crossbreeds and two razorbacks. Very near. They're angry now, because...because—"

Suddenly, his eyes flicked open and he favored me with another big grin. "Because they can't use me anymore!" he shouted. "Hallelujah! Praise God!"

I felt so good that I actually laughed then, and he joined me. For a moment or two, the only sound in that valley was our laughter, and if it sounded a mite hysterical, I figure we had every right. He was truly free. Whatever the hell mumbo-jumbo I'd done had worked.

As if on cue, we both stopped and looked at one another.

"Very near," I said, echoing what he'd told me.

David Jefferson nodded.

"Then we'd better scram, and quick."

He nodded again, and I shrugged on my pack, which held that old cap-and-ball, among other things, and picked up the rifle.

"C'm'on," I told him. "We've got one short stop to make on our way." The two of us hied it out of there in a fast trot for a couple hundred yards, until we ran onto a small creek. Moving as quickly as I could, I sloshed water on the Mannlicher, realizing that I did not have time to do a proper job of cleaning but knowing it would have to do. Once the action was cleared I was able to unload and reload it. They I blew through the barrel as hard as I could. David Jefferson stood thigh-deep in the water, watching me, occasionally looking back over his shoulder. He knew how close they were.

"What the hell," I cursed. I was hurrying too much to do a good job. And if our lives were going to depend on that Mannlicher —

Quickly, I dug into my pack, pitching stuff aside until I found my pull-through, which was nothing more than a string with a split fishing sinker on one end and a small bit of rag on the other. Dropping the weight through the muzzle, I caught at it as it reached the other end and pulled the rag through. It came out damp, which meant that the rifle could very easily have been out of commission if I hadn't done that.

However, this was hardly any time to congratulate myself on my foresight. "It's ready now," I told him, as I hurriedly shoved everything back into my pack and hoisted it onto my shoulders, holding the Mannlicher securely in my left hand. "My motorcycle is only about a quarter of a mile from here, I think."

As we began jogging away, he asked, "What's a motorcycle?"

John, he wasn't kidding. First that crack about 1877, then this. It was like he belonged to another time. (And it turns out he did. But once again I'm getting ahead of myself.)

I decided to take what he said at face value. I could always ask my own questions later.

"You'll see," I told him as we ran. "It's a machine that'll take us out of here. Once we get going, there isn't a pig alive that could catch us."

"That's real good," he returned. " 'Cause I think they're gaining."

Although it was still an hour or two before sunset, dusk had come to parts of the Ozark mountains, especially to the lower-lying areas, as the setting sun became blotted by the hills. Still, I was able to see the old road that led to the big Indian bike without any trouble.

Just as I spotted it, I heard over the sound of our running footsteps a sudden crashing and cracking in the brush behind us. David Jefferson turned his head toward the sound and then reached for my hand. When I grabbed it he took off like a scalded cat. It was like catching a box car going 30 miles an hour. He bounded through the brush toward the road with me hanging on for all I was worth, my feet hitting the ground only about every ten feet. I felt as though I were hanging on to the back end of a truck — he was that strong and fast.

We were right up on the tarpaulin-covered Indian before I knew it.

"This is it!" I shouted, and my companion ground to a stop, almost slamming me against the side of a hill in the process. I stepped to it and had my hands on the tarp when David Jefferson shouted, "Robert! Behind you!" and I turned just in time to see a black razorback flying toward me, spittle streaming.

I don't even remember drawing down on that pig; the Mannlicher seemed a part of me, moving of its own will as the pig's head exploded in a shower of gore.

"C'm'on!" I said, handing David Jefferson the Mannlicher and then breaking fingernails getting the Indian unwrapped; I'd never been as glad to see anything in my life.

With my passenger and everything else crowded into the sidecar, including that sawed-off shotgun of mine, I knew there wouldn't be any room for the tarp. So I let it lay and had David help me push the Indian up to the road and about fifty feet down it, hoping that would get enough gas and oil moving for everything to fire properly.

"Get in," I said, helping him into the side-car. If he had any trepidation about climbing into something he'd never seen before, he kept

it to himself. It was a tight fit, but he
managed to maneuver into the space pretty
quickly, especially for a man of his size. He
managed to keep hold of my rifle as he
settled in.

"Okay," I told him as I climbed on the bike.
"Stow the rifle now, David, and make sure the
shotgun's handy."

When he looked curiously at me, I added, "If
we've got to shoot any hogs at close range,
I'll have a better chance, a wider pattern,
with it."

"Yes," he nodded his understanding. "I'll
have my pistol ready, too."

"Good. Now say a prayer that I can get this
thing started."

"It had better be a short one," he returned.
"They are only a few hundred feet away."

Simultaneously, I heard more crashing in the
brush. They were just about on top of us.

"Well, shit," I muttered, turning the key —
and that sweet baby fired right off. At the
sudden burst of sound, David just about jumped
out of the sidecar, but he gritted his teeth
and gripped the edge of it hard with his free
hand.

"Hang on," I said, taking the shotgun from
him and maneuvering it across my lap.

He nodded, swallowed, and reached in his
pocket for his Colt. As we slowly picked up
speed — I couldn't gun it and take a chance on
killing the motor — I glanced over at him.
Instead of pulling out the .44, he'd gotten the

silver dollar, and he held it up, clutched between his thumb and forefinger, and gave me a grin.

"Now," he said, "I pray."

I nodded, then put all my concentration on steering us down that old logging trail to the county road, listening abstractly to David Jefferson's fervent, sonorous prayer for our strength and safety.

Then I heard the hog — just before I saw it. A huge gray-black Russian boar, as tall as the motorcycle and sporting big bayonet-like tusks, wet with glistening saliva. He broke into the trail suddenly, only a few feet ahead and to the right of us, and I let go a blast from the Mannlicher, the recoil almost knocking me off the seat. The animal flipped around and skidded on his side, on a collision course with us. Quickly, I goosed the Indian and we bounced forward as he slid past the rear tire, actually bumping it with that huge writhing body. If he'd connected any harder, he'd have flipped us over, but I couldn't dwell on what might have happened. Sticking the shotgun between David's leg and the inside of the sidecar, I concentrated on getting us the hell out of there.

With a last hard bounce we made the county road and the Indian bellowed as I let her out. It didn't take much imagination to hear that as a war whoop. I damn near joined in myself.

As we began to really pick up speed, a smaller black boar burst out of the woods in front of us. We were already moving faster than

he could run, but our trajectories might have
intersected if the razorback hadn't suddenly
reared and keeled over backward in mid-charge.

I'd heard the .44 go off beside me, and I
knew then that David Jefferson hadn't been
kidding about being "pretty fair" at shooting
targets from horseback. I nodded my apprecia-
tion, and he nodded back, his eyes scanning the
gathering dusk for any more signs of attack,
even as he continued holding onto the side of
the car in a death grip.

When we hit sixty I straightened up and
started to breathe again. That was about as
fast as I wanted to open her up. Those were
still mountain roads, with not a few hairpin
turns, and I had to be on my guard. Still, even
being careful, we made great time into Mackaville. Once or twice, we passed cars going the
other way, and it was almost comical the way
David followed them with his eyes. It was as
though he'd never seen an automobile before. I
had to believe that maybe he hadn't.

By the time we rolled into town, dusk was
edging into nightfall. And at about the time we
hit the city limits, every nerve in my body had
suddenly begun making like an aircraft siren.
Something was wrong — big wrong.

I'd planned to get David and me to Ma's and
hole up there, at least for a time, until I
could find out more about my companion and
what had happened up in those hills. I had
many questions for David, but the events that
had taken place since we'd met in that sink-

hole hadn't allowed for any deep conversations, and it was damned near impossible to understand more than a few words when the Indian was roaring anywhere near full-tilt. So the idea was to get David to a safe place and pepper him with questions until I was satisfied, and that safe place was the boarding house. I felt sure Ma wouldn't object to David's presence, even though he was Negroid, since as you know just about everyone in Mackaville — including Ma herself — seemed to be some part black.

Now, though, that plan went out the window. Somehow, in the time I'd been in the mountains, the town had changed. It felt as if we were riding headlong into an enemy encampment, hostile evil eyes peering out of every dark window, ready to attack us and rip us to tatters. I took side streets, telling myself it was because I didn't want to advertise David's presence in town, but I knew that was a lot of hooey. It took everything I had to keep from turning around and blasting back out into the hills, away from the prickly fear I felt simply from being back in Mackaville.

I had to think. If we headed back, who knows what would come after us. As long as I was on that big Indian, I had a target on my back. The Blacks would be after me, sure, but hell, those two oafs were the least of my worries. The hills held murderous entities that wanted to kill me — snakes, pigs, things that were part human and part animal, or animals directed by humans like Old Man Black and now, it seemed, the Gabbers.

Something had to be done to throw them off my trail. I wasn't safe in town, and I wasn't safe in the hills, and there were nothing but hills all around this accursed place. I might get through them to safety and freedom on the other side. But I might not.

Because of the noise of the Indian and the need for constant watchfulness on our trip through the mountains, David and I had hardly spoken to one another. But I'd tamped down the bike as we hit town, and through my agitation, I realized that David was speaking to me in low tones, saying something about how there'd been something wrong with the hogs we'd shot — that they hadn't been guided with much "power." I knew what he was saying was of interest, even significant, but I barely heard him. I was too busy trying to formulate a plan for our exit from this place. The alarm bells going off inside me didn't make thinking any easier.

Still, I got it figured out, almost in a flash. It would take three quick stops, and then out.

Praying a small prayer, asking God to give me the time I needed to pull it all together without being discovered, I maneuvered us around to a little hill just above Ma's boarding house and killed the Indian's motor. As we began to coast down, I reached over and put my hand over David Jefferson's mouth.

"Shhh, David," I said, just loud enough to

be heard over the rumble of the tires. "Save it and please tell me later."

He got the message.

It was maybe a hundred yards to the drive-way, and I coasted into the empty, open shed. There was no sign of Ma's car, so maybe I'd caught a break. I didn't want to have to explain myself to anyone.

"Get out and stretch your legs, but stay watchful," I whispered. "I'm going to get us some clothes and money. Then we're out of here." He nodded, and as I left, I heard the sound of empty shells being shucked out of the .44 as he began reloading.

John, I can't tell you if my seventh sense was still in charge or if it was just Robert blindly running headlong into — or, I mean, away from — something, which in this case was the whole damn town of Mackaville. I knew I had to get far away, and quick. The sense of oppression that had enfolded me when we'd hit town was almost overwhelming. What's more, I had a horrible feeling that maybe now I couldn't really trust anybody, not even my friends or fellow roomers. I tried not to accept that, but a wasp of doubt kept stinging at my brain, and as I crept to the house, I felt utterly and completely alone in the face of some enormous and sinister darkness.

I prayed it would stay quiet until I could get my stuff and leave. I fervently hoped no one was there in the darkened house — even my old pal MacWhirtle. I loved him, but I didn't think I could stand any yapping and barking in my current state. I hoped he was with Ma, wherever she was.

There seemed to be only one light burning. From the outside, it appeared to be the one over the kitchen sink that Ma often left on when she was away. Climbing the back steps, I slipped in the door — and something whirled in the kitchen.

Patricia.

She gasped when she saw me, and I quickly put a finger to my lips.

"Oh, Robert," she whispered urgently. "You have to go."

"Why? What's going on?" I whispered back.

Her eyes were saucers. "One of the Gabber brothers — they had to rush him up to Dodd General. I don't know why, but they're blaming you. I've been waiting here, to warn you in case you came back." She grabbed my shoulders, looking up into my eyes. "You didn't do anything to him, did you? Please tell me you didn't."

I shook my head. "Pat, on my honor, all I did was protect myself from some crazy pigs, up in the mountains."

But even as I said that, the seventh sense pulsed through me again, and I knew, somehow, I was responsible. The Gabber brother — I don't know, John, it was all mixed up and shooting through my head, but I suddenly had the distinct impression of human eyes, Gabber eyes, seeing through the pupils of pigs, and of the naked man I'd killed in the sinkhole. And then, David Jefferson's voice: "I feel them in my brain."

Patricia's voice brought me back to the present. "Pigs?" she whispered.

"Yeah." My voice had begun to rise, but I brought it down. "Where is everybody?"

"Ma is over at Grandmother's. The boarders have all eaten. I think Mister Clark is upstairs and the other two are in the living room, listening to the radio."

"I'll have to be quiet, then," I said. "I just need to grab some clothes and geetus and ankle this place for a while."

She swallowed, her hands still on my shoulders. "How can I help you?" she asked, and in that moment her voice was so guileless and disarming that I kissed her hard on the lips. She kissed me right back, and then I was headed up the back stairs, remembering where to step so as to not make any noise. A moment later, I was in my room, and I'd taken about three steps toward the chest of drawers when I suddenly cursed at myself for not looking out for snakes. Even though I had the whip hand on Old Man Black at the moment, it was an uneasy peace, and he was not exactly the trustworthy sort.

As it turned out, it wasn't what was in the room that gave me the shivers.

It was what wasn't.

I discovered the item's absence just as I was getting ready to leave the room. I'd thrown

open the drawers and taken out the railroad
overalls I'd bought at that second-hand store
in Harrison, the day I took the picture of the
little doll to send to Old Man Black. I'd also
grabbed a Pendleton shirt, a hand-me-down from
my old man. Both the shirt and the overalls
were plenty roomy for me; with a little luck,
they'd fit David Jefferson.

What about footwear? I'd wondered. I knew
none of my shoes would fit him. But maybe
galoshes? I'd found them in my closet and put
them in the pile with the shirt and overalls,
figuring they'd be better than nothing.

Then I'd skinned off my CCC uniform, folded
it and laid it into the suitcase, and gotten
into the dressy shirt and slacks I'd bought for
when Patricia and I went out, and thrown on a
jacket.

After that I bet I'd set some kind of record
for packing socks, shorts, and shirts into my
case. I'd cleaned out the top drawer and was
working on the second when I realized something
was wrong. I had some folding money stashed
back behind my underwear, and even though it
wasn't enough for what I had in mind, it would
be helpful.

When I pulled the drawer out farther I knew
someone had been there before me.

The little figure of Old Man Black. I'd
hidden it in the very back corner. But it
wasn't there anymore.

All right. Now I'm worn out enough to sleep,
I think. I'll put this in the mail tomorrow

morning and then try to take the rest of the day and tell you everything else — if I can. Hell, I might as well be writing a book.

Your pal and faithful comrade,
Robert

July 25, 1939
Tuesday morning

Dear John,

Just got back from the nearest St. Louie p.o., so in a few days you should have the first part of this epic saga in your hands. I've long since stopped worrying about whether you believe it or not (although I feel you do) or even why I'm writing it all down. I know I wrote you one time that I wanted you to have it all in case something happened to me. But hell, if something does, who'll believe all of this? Besides you, I mean.

All I can do is tell it, so I won't waste any more typewriter ribbon on omphaloskepsis, (When's the last time we used that word? I think it was maybe to describe old wool-gathering Mr. Floyd at Hallock High. I remember you're the one who found it in the dictionary.) and get right to it.

Knowing the little effigy was gone didn't do anything good for my nerves. Just another reason to get the hell out of town until I could think it all through. And, more immediately, to get the hell out of that room before any pigs or snakes or cats made an appearance. So I grabbed the overalls and shirt I'd set aside for David, clicked my suitcase shut, and moved, quiet but quick, out of my room and down the stairs.

Patricia was waiting. "Here," she said,

setting a paper sack on top of the clothes I held. "It's some food. I threw in a big chunk of baloney and some cheese and a box of crackers."

I couldn't think of anything to say, so, balancing the sack, I leaned in and kissed her again.

"Listen, Pat," I whispered, conscious that the boarders were in the building, "I want you to know that I didn't do anything directly to the Gabber boys. If anyone asks, you can say exactly that. I was attacked by hogs up in the hills, and I killed a hell of a lot of 'em, and maybe that has something to do with why one of the Gabbers is in the hospital. I don't know. I'm going to try to figure it out.

"What's important is that it was self-defense. Always. I didn't go looking for trouble. And whatever trouble I'm in now, I don't want it. Please believe that."

"I do, Robert," she said quietly. "But a lot of others here don't."

I made a face. "I know. Or I have an idea, anyway. And I can't help any of that right now. That's why I have to get away. But I'm coming back. Please believe that, too."

She nodded and tried a smile before wrapping her arms around me and kissing me again. From the living room, muted, came the sounds of a dance orchestra swinging out on "And the Angels Sing."

"I believe in you and I'll be here," she whispered past my ear. "Now go on."

I nodded, disentangled from her warm body, and beat it out the door and into the shed, where David stood beside the Indian. I handed him the Pendleton shirt and overalls.

"See if you can get into these," I said. "Quick."

He wasted no time, giving me the jacket to hold while he put on the shirt. "We had some visitors while you were inside," he said.

"What kind?"

"A couple of pussycats." He tried to button the front of the shirt, but it wouldn't quite come together. So, grinning, he left it open and stuck his feet into the overalls. At first, he got into them backward; it was like he'd never had any on before. I saw what he was doing and helped him negotiate the legs and the straps. Once we had him clad, I could see that the overalls barely contained him, but that was the best I could do. He looked at the galoshes quizzically before putting his feet in them. Lifting first one foot, then the other, he said, "I sent them away, though. The cats."

My skin prickled. "How?" I asked.

The grin didn't leave his face as he took the jacket back from me, put it on, and climbed in the sidecar. "I just gave them a reason to go elsewhere. Cats listen to reason, especially from — someone like me."

Son of a bitch, I thought. Just what I needed. Another human-animal, or animal-human, another denizen of this civilized jungle with power over its other inhabitants, both two- and

four-legged. And on top of it all, one that had
been around for a lifetime and didn't look much
older than I did.

Then again, what had I expected? After all,
I'd seen him go from pig to human — or I
thought I had — so I might as well believe the
whole business, at least until I could talk to
him a little bit more. Now, though, was not the
time. My buzzing senses told me to move, and I
did, firing up the bike and roaring out of the
shed, maybe feeling a little safer with David
Jefferson in the car beside me, and all the
mysteries about him be damned. But I still
could not shake that sense of doom that had
whipped over me like a shroud upon our entrance
to Mackaville.

I swallowed and headed for the second place
I needed to go before taking my run-out powder.
Even though it was still fairly early — my
strap watch said a little before eight — there
weren't many people on the streets. Still, I
kept the engine throttled down and slipped as
quietly as I could into the alley behind the
Castapolous Cafe. David climbed out, and I
found the camping pack in the sidecar, a little
misshapen from bearing some of the weight of my
passenger's big body.

"I'll be right back," I told him, hitting
the buzzer on Mr. Castapolous's back door.
"Knock if there's any trouble."

It took a few seconds, but suddenly the door
jerked open and there he was.

"Robert!" he said. "Get your ass in here!"

He pulled me in quickly and shut the door behind us.

"You know they're looking for you?" he whispered, nodding toward the door that separated his living quarters from his bar and diner.

"I've been told as much," I said, handing him the pack. "Some stuff in here you might be interested in. Take a look while I fetch your Mannlicher."

David stood by the bike, still as a sentry. He seemed to be pondering the sights around him, even though they were mostly just the shabby backs of stores, garbage cans stacked and spilling around the cobblestoned alley floor. I grabbed up the rifle, nodded at him, and went back through the door. Mr. Castapolous had dumped the contents of the knap sack on his kitchen table, and I could see he was nuts over the old .44 I'd found in the cave, as well as the powder horns. He held the cap-and-ball pistol almost reverently in both palms, whispering, "Beautiful... beautiful."

"It's yours," I said. "All I want to keep is this," and I picked up the little ledger book that I'd found with the gun and powder back in that cave, sliding it into my jacket pocket.

"But— but this— I can't," he sputtered, and I held up a hand.

"If it'd make you feel any better, I could use a loan. Some getting-out-of-town lettuce."

He grinned, and then sobered. "Yes?"

"I'll pay you back. Honest. I don't have quite enough saved to make it out on my own."

"It's a good idea. Something's going on. The pulse of this town, I feel it here in my cafe, and it's beating against you. Geetus, I got." He nodded toward an end table. I hadn't noticed before, but atop it was a thick stack of bills.

"I put it together for you, hoping you'd maybe come by before you left," he said. "Take it. Please."

I did. Tens and twenties, maybe a couple hundred simoleons. I stuffed them in my jacket, next to the ancient ledger book. "Thanks, Mr. Castapolous," I said. "You'll get every penny of it back."

He waved a hand. "No need. We're even." Caressing the pistol, he added, "This gun... she's worth it all to me." He looked up. "We talk when you return. Best for you to get the hell out of here now." He stuck out his hand to shake, but I grabbed that fat little Greek or Italian or whatever he is and hugged him. When I left, I thought I saw tears in his eyes, and I was damn close to weeping myself.

"Let's go," I told David, wheeling the bike around. Nodding, he got into the sidecar.

"See any more cats?" I asked him, kicking the big Indian to life.

"No more," he returned over the engine's roar. "Pigs, but they are miles away." He laughed, and his teeth were ivory in the darkness of the alley. "They do not seem to be able to sense me anymore. I expect they think I am dead. A good joke on them!" He was still laughing when we reached the mouth of the alley and headed out for my final destination: Pete's Skelly station. I took a roundabout route to try and keep from being discovered, every nerve in my body tingling, and I wondered if I was doing the wrong thing. Time was squeezing me like a noose, and I had no idea when and if it would make a final constriction. But I needed Pete for the last part of the plan that had begun forming in my mind the moment I realized I had to get out of town.

Could I trust him? Hell, of course. He was my friend. But still, this place had changed. Mr. Castapolous had it right — the pulse of the town, the blood thumping through its veins and arteries, had turned against me like the immune system turns against a disease that's trying to invade its body. That's what I felt like: A germ that had oozed its way into Mackaville's bloodstream and was just now being detected. The next step? Eradication.

On that cheery note, I pulled in behind Pete's place. He'd already turned off the pump lights, but there was still a dim glow inside his office.

I guess he heard the bike, even though it was running in low, because he came exploding out of the back door waving his hands, the most agitated I'd ever seen him. Pulling up the back of one of his garage doors, he nodded toward the darkened bay inside.

"Kill that son-of-a-bitch," he hissed as we rolled in.

I did.

He watched, and if he was surprised that I had someone with me, he didn't mention it. Maybe it had just been too dark for him to see much of anything, even though David was hard to miss.

As soon as we were in, Pete pulled the garage door back down, said, "Just a sec," and headed back to his office, clicking off the light. In a moment he was back. There were no windows in the bay, so when he shut the door it was dark as the inside of a cat. A moment later, the glow of a safe light shone from beside a work bench.

He looked from Jefferson to me and then said, in a hoarse whisper, "In the past coupla hours, I've had half the old folks in this town come by lookin' for you. Then Ma Stean called about seven. Said if I knew where you were to get hold of you and tell you to get your ass outta town. She didn't say 'ass' 'cause she don't cuss, but that was the general idea. I'll tell the world she was some upset."

"That's our plan," I said. "To get our asses out of town. But we need your help."

He seemed then to see David Jefferson for the first time.

"Hello," Pete said.

David nodded. "Hello," he returned, sticking out his hand. Pete shook it and turned to me with a questioning look he tried to disguise but failed.

"Pete Barlow," I said, "meet the Reverend Mr. David Jefferson. He's — well, I'm not

exactly sure <u>where</u> he's from, never mind <u>when</u>,
and if I told you how we met you wouldn't
believe it."

"You're a preacher?" Pete asked.

"I am now," David said. "Until Robert here
saved me, I had been a slave to the Gabbers.
For many, many years." He craned his neck,
taking in the tools and oil cans and the tires
stacked along the wall. "This is all for
carriages?" he asked.

Pete didn't even try to hide his astonish-
ment this time. Neither did I. It wasn't the
"carriages" comment, either. Suddenly, everything about David Garland Jefferson began
clicking into place. The pigs — and David, and
that human-pig companion accompanying him — had
been sent into the mountains by the Gabbers to
kill me. Why, I didn't know, but now I understood much more: Why the town had seemed so
toxic to me when we'd returned, what David had
meant about someone seeing through his eyes.
The Gabbers ran the packing plant, so they ran
the town. And if the Gabbers were against you,
it stood to reason that the town was against
you, too.

"About the Gabbers — was that what you were
trying to tell me when we were coming into
Mackaville?" I asked David.

"Yes. But I know you had other things on
your mind. There will be time to tell it all
once we are away from this place."

Pete then gave voice to some of my conclusions. "So this concerns the Gabbers," he said.

"That explains a lot. Gabbers run pretty deep in this town, and Jube Gabber's in the hospital under what you might call 'mysterious circumstances.' I get the idea that the townsfolk think you're responsible in some way. That wouldn't by any chance be true, would it?"

"Maybe," I admitted. "But I don't see how. All I did was shoot feral hogs." I tried not to let the image of the naked man into my thoughts.

"You're not making a whole lot of sense, Robert."

"I know. It's awfully complicated. For starters, you have to believe that people can change into pigs and back again, and that some other people — the Gabbers — can somehow see things through the eyes of their animals — that they can not only possess those beasts, but actually transform people into pigs." I nodded toward my companion. "That's what seems to have happened to David Jefferson here."

Before Pete could say anything, David asked, "Would you happen to be related to Uriah Barlow?"

Pete swallowed. "Why, sure," he said. "Uriah Barlow was my great-grandfather."

"He was my friend," returned David. "A good man. We rode together as Buffalo Soldiers. Tenth Cavalry."

There was silence for a moment as Pete pondered David's statement. Truth to tell, so did I.

"Then that would make you more than eighty years old," Pete said finally.

"I suppose," David told him. "I am not even sure what year this is."

"It's 1939," I said. "Should've told you earlier."

"Oh, my," David said softly. "My, oh, my."

His words settled into the darkness around us and no one said anything else for a moment. Then I jumped in.

"Pete," I said, fumbling in my jacket pocket and handing him some of the cash Mr. Castapolous had given me, "we've got to light a shuck out of Mackaville. I know there's a nine o'clock train goes through here every night to Little Rock." I checked my strap watch. "That's about 15 minutes from now."

"Sure. What do you want me to do?"

"Get over there and buy us two tickets. We'll take it from there. I'm afraid if I try to buy 'em I'm going to get spotted, and I can't afford that."

He nodded. "Why don't you do this," he said, following a moment's contemplation. "When that train pulls up, you two beat it around to the other side of the station and get up next to the door of the vestibule between the last car and next-to-last one. I'll get the tickets, climb on from the platform at the last minute, open the vestibule door, give you the tickets, and then hop off as she pulls away. That ought to do it."

Abruptly, Pete changed the subject. Looking

down at David's rubber-covered feet, he asked, "Why are you wearing galoshes, Preacher?"

David shrugged. "Robert gave this footwear to me."

"Take 'em off — at least one of 'em," Pete said, "and stick your foot up next to mine." Pete had on work boots, and David's foot matched his pretty well.

"I got you covered," he said, "thanks to these big gunboats of mine." Cracking open the door that led to his office, he pulled the safe light around so it shone on the floor outside, and he crept out. In a jiffy he was back with an old pair of work-worn brogans.

"Here," he said, handing them to David. "I keep these around for emergencies, and it looks like I've got one right here. Those galoshes'll have blisters rubbed on your feet before you can get 100 yards."

Thanking him, David didn't waste any time flipping off the rubbers and lacing up the shoes. Meanwhile, even though unanswered questions flickered through the air around us like fireflies, the knotting of my stomach and the shots of adrenaline exploding inside me told me it was time to move on, and fast.

"I'll leave the Indian here," I told him. "No one should spot it until you open up in the morning, and by that time we should be far away."

"All right," he said. "I'll throw a tarp over it. Any questions, and I'll just tell 'em you brought it back to its rightful owner."

A thought struck me then. "Listen, Pete. If I'm putting you in any danger—"

He cut me off with a wave of his hand. "You're the only one in danger, buddy," he said. "You and maybe the big preacher there."

"Okay," I said. "Thank you. We'd better go."

"Just a second," he said. "I've got something for you."

Cracking the door and repositioning the safe light, he walked to the register in the office. Nodding at David that everything was okey-dokey, I turned back around to find I was staring down the muzzle of a .38 revolver.

And there I will leave you hanging for a little while, as I muster up the energy to write about what happened next.

Your pal and faithful comrade,

Robert

July 25, 1939
Tuesday morning
(continued)

Dear John,

As I faced Pete and that pistol, I heard a quick and distinct click behind me. Pete's mouth dropped open, realizing that David had the drop on him with that .45 Colt Cavalry revolver Seth Black had given me.

"Relax, preacher," Pete said. "I just thought you fellas might need this." Flipping the pistol around his trigger finger, he held it out to me butt-first.

Although I was on high alert about every-thing and everybody in that town, I really wanted to believe that had been Pete's original intention, so I grabbed the gun and let my breath out in a gusty sigh.

"I think we're well-enough armed," I told him, and figured we were, what with the gun David was holding along with the .22 break-over pistol I'd gotten from my room. "But thanks anyway."

Pete grinned. "You didn't think I was going to hold you up, did you? Hell, I've already got your money." He flashed the bills I'd given him to purchase the train tickets.

I had to grin back. "Sorry, Pete. With all that's happened to us today, I'm just not sure about anything anymore."

"Buck up, kid. We'll get you outta here and

you'll be fine." He turned to David. "The two
of you get your plunder together and I'll bring
my car around to the back. You'll hear it.
Don't waste any time once you do."

"Yes, sir," David said.

Pete left then, and we got our baggage out
of the sidecar. It was only the suitcase and my
pack, which now contained the food Patricia had
put together for me. I pulled out a manila
envelope with those two letters I'd handwritten to you while I was still up in the
mountains. I'd already put your name and
address on it, leaving the return address
blank. Licking the seal flap, I pressed it shut
and held onto it. Then I handed David the suitcase and a little bit of Mr. Castapolous's
money.

"Here," I said. "You can carry this, and
you take this money. I'm sure we won't get
separated, but if we do, you'll need some
cash."

He took the bills, glanced at them, and
stuffed them in the jacket pocket that also
held the .45.

"Money has changed a great deal," he
observed.

Before I could say anything in response, I
heard the rumble of Pete's '36 Hudson outside
the bay. "Let's go," I said to David, and we
headed out the side exit, where the car was
waiting. Jerking the back door open, I told
David over my shoulder to put the suitcase in.
Then I turned to see him standing there, suit-

case dangling from one big hand, a look of stunned trepidation on his face.

"I saw many of these in town, stopped, and some on the road, moving," he said. "But never was I this close."

"You're going to get a lot closer," I said, laughing despite our plight. "Put the suitcase in the back. It's okay. Trust me."

Muttering something, he set the case on the back seat, and I followed with the pack, keeping the manila envelope with me. Then I got in the front, sliding over to the middle.

"C'm'on," I said, patting the part of the seat beside the door with my hand. With some reluctance, he got in next to me, and I reached across him and shut the door. Even though the Hudson was plenty roomy, we were all three packed together in that front seat, and I was so close to David that I could feel him trembling a little. John, you could hardly blame the guy. If what he said was true, he'd suddenly been thrust fifty years ahead, into the twentieth century. It must've been like diving into ice water.

Give him credit, though. Before we even had covered the few blocks to the station, his trembles had stopped and he was busy glimming the sights through the windshield of the Hudson.

Later on, he told me getting in that car was one of the hardest things he ever did.

It only took us minutes to get to the depot, and even then we were cutting it close. The

train was already at the station, a few passengers straggling out onto the platform. Pete
pulled in as close as he could get to the
caboose and said, "All right. Get around there
and I'll see you in a jiffy."

"Here," I said, handing him the envelope.
"Could you mail this for me?"

"Sure."

"There's no return address. That's inten-
tional. I don't trust the postmaster. I wrote
the address in all capital letters, and if you
mail it, he might not get the idea it came from
me, and it'll go where it's supposed to go."

"All right," he said, "but—"

"Thanks," I said, and again reaching across
David, threw open the door.

I have to admit that as we bailed out and
began running around to the off side of the
train, I couldn't shake a lingering doubt about
Pete. He was a part of the town, after all, and
between what Pat and Mr. Castapolous had told
me and my seventh sense, I knew the town had
now turned on me like a single living organism.
It would be easy for him to rat us out and get
us caught by the bulls and hauled back in. I
knew from past experience that the Mackaville
cops were no chums of mine, and at this point I
was so mixed up I wasn't sure if I could even
trust Sheriff Meagan. After all, in the after-
math of my dust-up with the Black twins, hadn't
he said something about how he wasn't always
going to be able to pull my fat out of the
fire?

And then there was Patricia. Another, even more unsettling thought skittered across my mind then. Was I putting her in danger? When they couldn't get me, would they go to her? True, she was one of them, but she was also my girl, and lots of people knew it. What if, what if, what if—?

I turned my attention to the train. David and I ran beside it, with him taking a cue from me and keeping low so that we wouldn't be seen in the light from the windows. In a moment, we'd reached the first vestibule from the end car.

"This is it," I whispered. "Keep an eye out. And you might send up a prayer, too."

He nodded.

It was pretty dark on that side of the tracks, but I could just barely see the second hand on my strap watch, with what seemed like an eternity of waiting between each little click. The sudden cry of the train whistle made us both jump, and as the cars jerked into motion, I was struck with an overwhelming sense of doom. Pete wasn't coming. We were stranded there, to be exposed once the last car pulled out of the station.

What happened next made it obvious that whatever had given me that harrowing notion sure as hell wasn't my seventh sense. In a flash, the vestibule door opened and there was Pete, tickets in hand. Hustling David in, I grabbed the tickets and was barely able to thank him before he'd slapped my shoulder,

said, "See ya 'round, kid," and hopped off into
the darkness.

The train lurched, and David and I began
making our way through the vestibule toward the
front of the train. The anxiety was leaving me
in waves now, and I didn't see the porter until
he was right in front of us.

"Where you boys think you're goin'?" he
asked, a little belligerently for my tastes.

"We have tickets," I told him, holding them
out. He didn't even take them.

"Yes, I see that," he said. "But if you
travelin' with this boy" — he nodded at David —
"best be gittin' yo' asses back in the colored
car."

Oh, yeah. I'd forgotten for a moment we were
in dear old Dixie.

Well, the last thing I wanted to do was
cause a scene before we'd even gotten out of
Mackaville, so I started to turn around,
knowing the "Jim Crow" car — Lord, how I hate
that term — was the last in the line. But
before I knew it, David had grabbed the porter
by his uniform front and shoved him up against
the side of the vestibule so hard that the wood
work gave out a creak.

"No black man calls me boy," David whispered
harshly, his face only an inch or two from the
porter's. "You want to speak to me, you speak
right, and no shit. You can call me Reverend,
or you can call me Sergeant. You don't call me
boy. Got it?"

"Yassuh, Reverend Sergeant," the man said quickly. "Yassuh."

David released the porter and, after giving him another stern look, followed me down the short vestibule to the end car. Grinning in spite of myself, I threw open the door and stepped in, David just behind me.

John, it was just like one of those B-budget saddle operas when the hero pushes open the swinging doors and strides into the saloon — and the piano player suddenly stops and every conversation screeches to a halt. I'd opened the door onto a lot of boisterous conversation, but as soon as we entered it died, hanging in the air like the haze of cigar and cigarette smoke that drifted around the seats and above the heads of the passengers.

I knew it was me. I might have a pretty dark tan, and I might have kept my cap on because my red hair wouldn't have helped me to "pass" for colored, but everyone in there knew I didn't belong. Their eyes on me, male and female, said it all.

Then, David stepped in and laid a massive hand on my shoulder. "Good evening," he rumbled in his stentorian preacher's voice. A few of our fellow passengers replied softly to him. Others just continued staring.

David smiled. "We're glad to be with you," he said in the same tones and with a subtle push against my spine urged me onward. The car was a little over half full, with the first empty seat four rows down. I paused beside it.

"If it's all the same to you, I'd prefer the aisle side," I said softly.

"Maybe I'd better have it, Robert. If it's all the same to you," he echoed. I nodded and slid across the seat to the window. We were on his ground now; he knew best.

With our meager luggage between us on the long wooden seat, we settled in as the train began its looping ascent into the mountains around Mackaville. As soon as we'd cleared the boundaries of the city, the adrenaline that had been coursing through my system for the past few hours leaked out of me like air out of a balloon, and I was suddenly very tired. I had my eyes closed, letting myself be lulled by the motion of the train, when the conductor, a gruff old Caucasian with a three-day growth of beard, came by for the tickets. I passed them to David, they were duly punched, and he stuck them in the pocket of the Pendleton.

While my body was experiencing the letdown of complete fatigue, a part of me wanted to keep awake and instead talk to David, to ask him the questions that had been bubbling around in my brain in the incredible hours since I'd seen my companion transform — or so I thought — from hog to man and then from foe to ally. His references to the Gabbers, his obvious unfamil- iarity with the present day — I needed to know about it all, I needed to try hard to under- stand, no matter how unbelievable it might be.

It would've been a damn sight more unbe- lievable if I'd been some wet-behind-the-ears kid with just enough education to poo-poo anything that couldn't be explained by rational means.

I don't have to tell you that I hadn't been that guy for a long time. You know from my letters that I've seen things, the kinds of things that change your thinking forever.

That battle between giving in to blessed rest and bracing David with a few questions was raging in me when a voice came from beside us. "Gentlemen," it said.

I looked up to see the porter, fresh from his dust-up with David. He was carrying a couple of cardboard cups full of coffee, and it smelled damn good.

"You b— fellas look a little used up, you don't mind my sayin' so," he told us. "Thought you might like you a coupla cups a' joe."

"Sure," David said, taking the steaming containers from him and passing me one. "We are much obliged."

"Lissen," the porter began, looking around and lowering his voice. "About out there—" He nodded toward the vestibule.

"Done forgotten," David said. "What do we owe you for the coffee?"

"On th' house. Cook's a friend of mine."

The car had gotten quiet again. Taking a sip of the welcome but practically boiling brew, I could see that everyone was watching this exchange. For some reason — maybe David's size, or the fact that they weren't sure about my negritude, or even the difference in looks between the two of us — we were squarely under the spotlight.

"Well, then," said David, reaching in a front pocket of the Pendleton, where he'd put the money I'd given him, and giving the car a sweeping glance that took in all the gazing faces, "why don't you see if anyone else wants a cup? And you can keep the change." He pulled out a dollar bill and magnanimously handed it to the porter, who looked from the bill to David's face.

"Uh... they charges a dime a cup on the trains," he said, gulping. "They may be more'n ten folks here'd like coffee."

David chuckled and added two more bills. "All right. This should take care of it. And you still keep the change." He looked around and raising his voice, said, "Anyone here want a cup of coffee on me and my friend?"

In the general din that followed, I leaned across and whispered, "You're getting awfully free with my money, Reverend Sergeant Jefferson."

He just grinned.

I guess buying a round for the house, even when it's coffee, breaks down barriers better than just about anything else. The car erupted in conversation again, and as we were on a relatively level stretch of tracks now, people were up and roaming around, coming by and asking about us, where we were from, that sort of thing. Once the coffee came, most of the passengers sat back down in their seats to enjoy it, and I thought that might be my time to play twenty questions with David, but then an older portly high-yellow guy in a rumpled brown suit came by and sat down on the edge of the empty seat across from us.

"I am Lawrence Thomas," he said, sticking out his right hand while clutching the coffee container with his left. We shook hands and gave him our names. "I'm a drummer," he continued. "Been working my route down to Dallas and I'm now headed home to St. Louis. How 'bout you boys? Where you going?"

I glanced at David to see how the "boys" had gone over, but he seemed to have taken no offense. St. Louis, I thought. Might be nice.

"That's where David and I are bound," I said. "We've never been, and we've heard a lot about it, so we thought: why not?"

David may have been surprised about our destination, since we hadn't discussed it. But if he did, he sure didn't show it.

"That's right, Mr. Thomas," he said. "We figured a big city might be a nice change."

"Well, now, that's just fine. What you boys do?"

"Preacher. AME," David said.

"Writer," I told him.

"He's my second cousin," David added, smiling paternally at me. For everything he was suddenly having to deal with, he'd maintained a damn good sense of humor.

I sat back, finishing the last couple of swallows of my coffee, and watched as a few others gathered around and began talking with David and Mr. Thomas like they were all lodge brothers. After downing a cup of java that robust I should've been wide awake, but I was inexorably relaxing after the events of the past couple of days and I closed my eyes, letting the exhaustion take over. I was tumbling into the warm vortex of sleep when I got the feeling there were eyes on me, and reluctantly I opened my peepers to find a little black girl maybe four years old standing in the seat right in front of us, looking me over. When she saw my eyes open she piped right up.

"You white, mister?" she asked guilelessly.

The woman beside her turned her bandana-wrapped head around with disapproval. "Now, Marcella," she began. "Leave that man alone."

I smiled. "It's okay," I told her. And then, to the little girl: "No, honey," I said. "I'm mixed."

She was perfectly happy with that answer, turning around and sitting back down beside the woman I figured was her mother. For my part, I felt as though a load had been lifted. I hadn't ever thought before about how important it is to be accepted. And really, I hadn't lied. We're all mixed. Just a bunch of different mixtures.

And with that thought spinning around in my mind, I leaned my head against the window and let myself be pulled into the vacuum of sleep — only to be jerked back out by my nerves, my

seventh sense, humming like a hive of bees. The
radium dial of my strap watch told me it was
near midnight, which meant I'd been out for
hours. Everybody else in the car seemed to be
sleeping as well, even David, his big head
lolling on the back of the seat, rolling with
the movement of the train, his breathing as
deep and heavy as his preacher's voice.

A guy was creeping through the vestibule
door, a white man in a shabby gray suit.

I knew it was all wrong.

Following him with my eyes, I saw him step
up beside our seat and reach across to tap me
on the head. I jerked away before he could
touch me, and he grinned, showing teeth that
looked scummy even in the dimness of the car.

"Good. You're awake," he whispered. "Come
with me, sucker, and be quiet about it. Hate to
see anyone get hurt — 'specially you." He
emphasized his words by moving the obvious
muzzle of a gun through the taut fabric of his
jacket pocket.

I nodded and rose, working my way past
David's knees, a gut-wrenching sense of danger
pinwheeling around inside me. As I passed
David, wondering how to make him aware of the
situation without getting us both shot, he
subtly but unmistakably tapped me with one
knee. That made me feel considerably better.

The man waited for me in the aisle, stepping
behind me and jabbing the gun in my back. "Take
it easy, buddy," he hissed. "You're getting off
here."

I figured we were doing about sixty miles an hour, so his plan didn't have much appeal to me. He gave me another good poke with the gun as I pulled open the vestibule door, and then it shut behind me, and I heard a sudden hissing noise, followed by a kind of cracking, like you might hear if someone crumpled a couple of those little wooden boxes strawberries come in. First one, and then another. The pressure of the gun left my spine, and I turned to see that David had crept up behind us and reached around the guy, grabbing his weapon. All I could see under David's big hand was a tiny bit of gun barrel, splattered with rivulets and spurts of crimson.

That was where the sound of the first crushed strawberry box had come from. When I stepped away, I glimmed the source of the second. David had the little weasel by the back of the neck, squeezing. The man's eyes bulged from his sockets, his tongue from his mouth, and the pitiful attempts he was making at shouting sounded instead like death rattles. Then a stench hit me and I realized he'd crapped in his pants. I knew that happened when someone—

"Open that door," David said, nodding to indicate which one he meant.

No sooner said than done. I held it open against the pressure of the wind, and David, never letting go of the guy's neck, grabbed his belt, gave him a heave, and then all that was left was the smell, which quickly dissipated, following its creator out the door and into the rushing darkness. Remarkably, even in death, he'd apparently managed to hold onto his gun, if not his bowels.

Neither of us said anything as we crept back to our seat. It wasn't until we were settled and my heart had begun slowing down when David leaned across and whispered, "Ain't you glad I had the aisle side?"

Like I wrote you before: For all he'd been through, the man's sense of humor was certainly admirable. I don't know, though, if I could've been that cavalier after killing a man.

Your pal and faithful comrade,

Robert

July 26, 1939
    Wednesday morning (<u>early</u>)

Dear John,
    I woke up this morning before dawn thinking
I was back in that Jim Crow car, next to David
Jefferson, the lingering smell of human excre-
ment in my nostrils. But in the dream I awak-
ened from, the smell stood for something else.
You know how things change when you're dream-
ing, how symbols and senses and images get all
mixed up and become different entities with
different relationships? I know I'm not
explaining this right; dream logic is hard to
pin down. I wish I had old Carl Jung here to
throw a light on it. But I don't, so the best
way I can get it across is to tell you this:
while the odor I thought I smelled was that of
a dead man's final desperate bowel evacuation,
what the smell <u>meant</u> was the Gabbers.
    I think it was something I'd known even
while David was working that poor bastard over
in the train. My seventh sense told me that the
guy had been sent by the Gabbers, sure as hell,
although I'm still not clear why they want to
kill me. Of course, it has something to do with
David and the hogs. He's told me just enough
for me to understand that, to validate the
feeling I've had since my night in the cave.
I'm not entirely clear about it all yet, but
I'm going to be. David is the key, and I've

asked him if we can have a conference, just the two of us, later today.

You may be wondering, what the hell? Especially if you've read the batch of letters I sent off yesterday. If you calculate correctly, you'll know that David and I met up four whole days ago. So why haven't I talked to him at length and maybe gotten things cleared up in my own mind about him and the hogs and the Gabbers?

Here's why:

After the incident on the train — and more about that in a minute — we both fell exhaustedly asleep. And while the jouncing of the car on the tracks kept me from falling too deeply into the arms of Morpheus, I dove into unconsciousness enough to experience a series of crazy, fluid dreams. I guess all my adventuring of the past couple of days had finally caught up with me; when it came time to switch trains at Little Rock, I could barely wake up enough to understand I needed to move. I have an impression of David propping me up like I was some drunk, and then plopping me down onto a seat. I think my eyes were open, but that's about all I remember. It was dark, and the damn car we alighted looked and smelled to me exactly like the one we'd just left.

It must've been very early Sunday morning when we arrived in St. Louis. I guess David and Mr. Thomas, the salesman returning home from Dallas, had talked more and become pals in the bargain, because the old drummer took us across

town on the trolley cars to his boarding house
and got us set up with a room. That's where I'm
writing you from. But I can't tell you much
about our checking in because I was still stumbling around like one of those characters in
Revolt of the Zombies. In fact, all I remember
doing that first morning was dropping my bags
on the floor and climbing into bed.

Like I say, I was worn to a frazzle after
all that had happened. But there was something
else, too. In this place, hundreds of miles
away from Mackaville and all its threats and
weirdness, I felt safe and secure for the first
time in a long time, and I dropped off to sleep
like I'd stumbled off the top of a cliff into a
pool of midnight.

I was out cold until supper time. Maybe it
was the smells that brought me back to the land
of the living. Whatever it was, I managed to
get dressed and stumble downstairs, just in
time to see the lady that owns and runs the
place, Mrs. (or Miz) Evans, rolling out the
grub for her boarders, a party of eight that
included both David and Mr. Thomas, who greeted
me warmly.

So did Miz Evans. A nice lady of only
slightly ample proportions, she gave out with
some entertaining lines comparing me to
Sleeping Beauty and how she was going to have
Mister Jefferson put a mirror under my nose to
see if I was still breathing.

Apparently, she and Mister Jefferson were
already getting along quite nicely. I had no

idea how much he'd slept, but clearly he'd done a lot less of it than I had, and a lot more getting acquainted. Groggy as I was, I could see there was a lot of bonhomie surrounding him and the other boarders — not to mention Miz Evans. She hauled in a huge plate of fried chicken, and when one of the guys (her boarders are all men) reached out for a piece, she whacked him on the wrist with the back of her serving fork.

"You know what Mister Reverend Jefferson said," she said, nodding toward David. "Let's have us a little manners and wait for grace — 'specially in front of Mister Reverend Jefferson's white friend. An' on a Sunday, too."

I imagine I blushed visibly at the "white friend" remark, but I was too tired to worry much about it. As it turned out, I was hungry, too, even though the food was a little unusual to me. Following David's succinct prayer, the chicken went around, then a dish called "Hoppin' John," which is beans and rice with ham hocks for flavor. Also, we had collard greens, which I'd had at Ma Stean's, and stewed okra and tomatoes. Not exactly dishes my Minnesota palate was familiar with, but I developed a taste for 'em pretty damn quick. Dessert was a peach cobbler, which was different from the ones we're used to because it had both a top and bottom crust. You would love it.

I scored points with the others by leaving the ham hocks in the Hoppin' John and taking only two pieces of chicken, the neck and, as my

old Indian uncle used to say, "the piece that
went under the fence last."

"Don'tcha need more yard bird than that?"
Miz Evans asked me.

"No, ma'am," I said. "I'll leave it for the
men who are working hard. I write for a living,
and that doesn't take much fuel."

That got a friendly laugh, which made me
feel pretty good. David, sitting on my left,
slapped me on the shoulder. "Nice to have you
up and around," he said.

"Thanks," I returned. For the first time I
noticed that he had on a new dark blue cotton
shirt. "Looks like you found some better
clothes to wear."

"My late husband, rest his soul, had some
that fit Mister Jefferson good," said Miz
Evans. "They both just about the right size."
The way she emphasized "right" further justi-
fied my suspicions about the relationship
between David and our landlady. For a guy from
the 19th century, it looked to me like David
Jefferson wasn't having any trouble with the
intricacies of modern-day romance.

For his part, David just smiled.

"Excuse me," said a voice on my other side.
I turned to see a young, bespectacled man, very
black and very serious-looking.

"Yes?"

"Did you say you were a writer?"

"That's right. I'm with the WPA Folklore
Project."

He nodded. "I know about that. I've put in

for the Federal Writers' Project. I, uh, write. Poetry mostly, but I've been trying to do some prose, too."

"Well, then, we'll have to talk shop," I said, "I'm not much of a poetry expert, but good writing is good writing."

He nodded again, as though what I'd told him had great import, before solemnly sticking out his hand. "My name's Richard," he said. "And I'd like that. Shop talk, I mean. But it would have to be in the evening or Sunday. I have a mail-clerk job during the day."

"That's fine. And I'm Robert."

"I know. You've been the talk of the place."

Then, the bowl of collard greens came my way again and I fell into listening to the small talk around the table as I shoveled food into my mouth at a pretty good clip. When my hunger finally began to slake, I found myself getting leaden again, and it was all I could do to keep my eyes open through the cobbler. I was glad when the gathering broke up and, just like at Ma's, several of them headed into the living room, where a rumble of voices came from the radio. Fuzzy as I was, I'd had thoughts of taking David aside for some questions, but then I saw him standing there with his head cocked, a big grin on his face, right in front of Miz Evans' big Atwater Kent floor model.

I realized then he had come from a world without radio. I didn't know when he'd discovered it — maybe just a few hours ago — but what a jolt it must've given him. And now, like

millions of other Americans across the country,
including most of our fellow boarders, he was
laughing along with Jack Benny and his Jell-O
program.

I didn't want to deprive David of that plea-
sure, so I found my way up the stairs with the
idea of plopping back into bed. However, when I
heard the stair creak behind me I turned to see
Richard.

"Excuse me," he said self-consciously. "Are
you busy now?"

"No. A little sleepy, though."

"Then maybe another time."

He unconsciously glanced down at a few pages
of folded-up paper in his hand, and there was
something about the gesture that told me what
he wanted.

"Got some of your poems there?" I asked.

He nodded, looking down.

"Hell, I'm not _that_ sleepy," I told him.
"Come on up. I'd like to hear 'em."

So he did, and they were damn good. As you
know, I'm not exactly an expert on poetry, but
these struck me as almost classical in their
structure, rhyming instead of free verse, with
some good if kind of tortured imagery. Richard
seemed a little nervous about sharing them, but
since he saw me as a fellow writer I guess he
figured I'd be a good audience. We talked a
little bit after he read them to me, but I was
getting progressively more sleepy, and, sensi-
tive fellow that he is, he saw I was flagging
and made his exit. Before he got away, I made a

deal with him to use his typer, since mine is back at Ma Stean's. The arrangement we have is for me to take it during the day and let him have it at night. I insisted on giving him a dollar bill for the paper and ribbon I'd be using, and although he protested a little, he finally took the buck and seemed grateful for it.

I woke up rested and early the next day, Monday, and started this series of opuses to you. I'm trying to give them to you in digestible lengths, but the wordage is also determined by how many I can do before I have to stop and relax for a while. I'll probably knock out another installment later on today.

Your pal and faithful comrade,

Robert

P.S. Looking back over this letter, I see that I said I'd write about the "incident" with the gunman and the train. I approach the subject with serious reservations, because it forces me to see my friend David Jefferson in a different light, and after what we've been through together I'm reluctant to do that.

But a writer's allegiance is supposed to be to the truth — that's one of the things young Richard said last night, and he's right — so here it is: In that vestibule only a few days ago, right before my eyes, David Jefferson turned into a killer beast, one that savagely took a life with little if any compunction. Now you know me well enough to know that I'm not talking like a Klansman or one of those Black

Legion thugs, about how Negroes are little more than animals and all that hateful crap. David Jefferson is a man like you and me, no less and no more.

Or maybe "no more" isn't right. Could it be possible that he still possesses some wild animal tendencies from his long stretch of enslavement in a feral hog's body? And that those predilections all came out when he saw me threatened by that poor dumb goon?

I haven't broached him yet about our "conference." But I will, and soon, and I hope like hell I have the guts to ask him about that.

July 27, 1939
Thursday morning

Dear John,

I thought I would be writing more yesterday, but after finishing the letter I found myself getting awfully sleepy again, so I stretched out on my bed and the next thing I knew it was suppertime. Maybe it was the soporific effects of Miz Evans' breakfast — fatback, which is a kind of thick bacon, biscuits, and cream gravy — or it could have been, as I wrote earlier, the pervasive sense I had that there was now no threat lurking around me and I could rest in peace. (Considering all that's gone on, maybe that's not the best phrase to use.) For whatever reason, as Shakespeare wrote in <u>Hamlet</u>, sleep has knitted the raveled sleeve of care, and I feel great right now — even after having what became a pretty intense "conference" with David Jefferson last night. Sure, I'll tell you about it shortly.

I plan on mailing these latest missives — four, counting this one — this afternoon, and when I take the trolley to the post office I'm going to stay downtown and look around a little, find out what St. Louis has to offer besides the Cardinals and all those hitters they've got. I'll bet I can find a second hand bookstore somewhere, for sure a newsstand with pulps. But before I do all that, I want to catch you up, and in looking over the letters

I've written beginning Tuesday, I see they've only talked about the 22nd and the 23rd, with nothing at all about this past Monday, Tuesday, and Wednesday.

Truth to tell, there hasn't been much to write about — until yesterday evening. I mostly wrote you and slept and ate Monday and Tuesday. I know I'm going to have to return to Mackaville and finish my job before I can move on to Washington, even though the thought of it makes my stomach clutch up, but for right now I feel that I'm home among these good colored people, who are treating me like one of their own. After Miz Evans' crack Sunday night about how I was David's "white friend," no one else has brought up anything about race, which is fine with me. For long stretches I forget that they're Negroes and I'm a Caucasian, even though their food and their way of talking and maybe even looking at life is a little different. I suppose if I were going to be here longer I'd see more and more differences.

But different doesn't mean worse — or better, for that matter. When you get down to it, we're all different in one way or another. Aren't we?

David's different. That's for sure. He's not only from another race, but another time. I wrote earlier that he and Miz Evans seemed to be hitting it off, and I've seen nothing since that would change my mind. However — and this leads to the most important part of this letter — I did manage to take him aside just after dinner last night and ask him if we could have a talk.

He understood immediately. "Yes," he said. "That would be a good thing. We are due."

"When?" I asked.

He glanced wistfully at the living room, where most of the others were settling themselves into chairs and a big overstuffed sofa around the radio. Then he shrugged. "I guess it should be now," he said, and as if on cue, the two of us went upstairs to our shared room. Closing the door, he pulled up a wooden chair and sat down. I did the same, right in front of the scarred desk with Richard's typewriter atop it.

"David," I began. "Soon I'll have to go back to Mackaville and finish my job, even though I know it'll put me in more danger. I don't much want to go back, but I have to. You know things that might help me survive, and I hate like hell to ask you the questions I have, but I must."

I couldn't read his expression, but I saw agony in it.

He nodded. "I knew we would have to have this talk, Robert. It will be very...unpleasant for me to talk about it, but I owe you too much to hold it back. And you are my friend."

"I am."

David took a deep breath, his big hands clasping and unclasping. And when he began speaking, he didn't look at me.

"Please understand I do not know everything.

But I do know and will never forget the horror that descended on me and my family," he said, and the hair on my arms rose at his words. "I did not know anything was coming until that night. The fire bell in town began ringing, then stopped. I told my wife to stay in bed and I got up, dressed, and rushed outside. They were waiting for me. I was clubbed down."

He swallowed, still looking toward the floor.

"It was almost a day before I came around, and by that time it was all over. I was in the packing plant, surrounded by armed men, and when they saw I was conscious they dragged me into a room where the Gabbers were waiting."

"The same Gabbers? When was this?"

"The same Gabbers," he said, finally looking up at me. "In 1889."

I started to ask how that could be, but the anguish on his face and his tearful eyes told me I'd be better off just listening. So I nodded and he continued.

"The Gabbers informed me that because of who I was, a religious leader in the community, a preacher, but most of all a relative, the council had decided that I must not be killed. And what they decreed was much worse than death. It was the purgatory of my servitude to the Gabbers as a wild animal that lasted until you rescued me. I lived for decades as you found me. Not human, not dead, not even aging — but in Satan's own hell."

A single tear ran down his ebony cheek.

"They slaughtered my family. They slaughtered many others. They told me this. But they didn't tell me all of it.

"I don't know how many others died that night in 1889, but over the many, many years, in the times when I was allowed to take human form, I heard stories of the mass killings. Many times, I've wished I could've been one of their victims."

My mind flashed back to that mass grave that included Mrs. Davis's husband, with the 1889 date, and I knew firmly and irrevocably what David was talking about.

"These mass murders... Was that what was known as the Cleansing?"

"I— yes. Yes. I have spent most of my life as...as an animal, but I could hear human speech, and understand it."

That fantastic <u>animal</u> comment caught my attention and raised any number of other questions, but I was hell-bent to get to the bottom of the Cleansing first.

"Why, David?" I asked. "Why all the killing? Who was behind it? The Gabbers?" I believe that last sentence came courtesy of my seventh sense, although a lot of other things I'd learned pointed to it. David Jefferson stared wordlessly at me for a few moments, and when he spoke again he was actually shaking. I got a glimpse then of how hard it was for him to relive this, to tell someone else about it for what had to be the first time ever. Then his eyes, filmed with unshed tears, locked with mine.

"Robert," he said, "there is something so evil in that town. You can't begin to understand the magnitude of it. Believe me. You go back, you may die. Or worse."

I knew he wasn't kidding, but I needed more information. When I started to speak, however, he seemed to change before my eyes, the abject despair in his eyes giving way to a mounting rage. Suddenly leaping from the chair like an animal, he grabbed me by the front of my shirt, twisted it, and pulled my face to his. His reddened eyes gleamed in the lamplight of the room, and they were the eyes of that huge boar up in the mountains, staring down at me as I looked up from that damn sink hole.

"Do not forget this," he hissed. "You are crazy to go back to that place. I hope you live. But whatever you do there to survive, do not lift a hand to the Gabbers. Do you understand?"

Shocked as I was, I only managed to stammer out a "Yes, but—" before he spoke again.

"The Gabbers are mine to settle with. Mine and mine alone."

I managed to nod, and he let go of my shirt front and stood there, panting. There was a struggle going on inside him. It may have been between man and beast, or, in the time-honored tradition, between the bestial and the spiritual, but David's internal battle etched itself on his twitching face. It moved through him like electricity, like careening worms under his skin.

We stood there like sculptures, the two of us, until David gradually slowed his breathing. His eyes had never left my face, and mine had never left his. All I could think was that I'd gotten an answer about the beast within him without ever having to ask the question.

"I'm sorry, Robert," he whispered. "The Gabbers kept me alive, if you could call what I experienced a life, after executing everyone I loved. They killed my whole world and kept me alive to watch. And as God is my witness" — his voice raised, rang out — "my brothers will pay with their lives!"

Brothers? I thought. The Gabbers are his brothers?

Then, he sat back down and, over the course of the next hour, gave me the story as best he could remember it. And while I'm going to relay it to you as briefly as I can, because, God willing, there'll be time for details later, you'd better be sitting down. It is a fantastic story. Perhaps it's a fanciful one. But I don't think so. Given my experiences so far in and around Mackaville, what David told me makes frighteningly perfect sense.

It started in the early to mid-1800s — David was unsure of a specific date — when the town's founder, a fellow named MacKenzie, bought a whole boatload of African slaves and moved them to the site of what became Mackaville. He was in the meat-packing business, which was still fairly new then, and he bought up a lot of land cheap and started a packing plant in that isolated spot in the Ozarks. There was a lot of slave labor in Arkansas at the time, working cotton fields and the like, but what made MacKenzie's slaves different is that they came from three different, but nearby, parts of the Congo, and each had an animal totem.

So far, all of this synched up with what Pete had told me when we'd had our lunch together up in the mountains back several weeks ago, the day we'd later hit that rope stretched across the road. But David's account was brimming with detail.

The most powerful of these slaves belonged to the pig tribe, whose members had the ability to change people into pigs — or, at least, put their spirits into those animals. David wasn't exactly sure which it was, but he knew that when it happened, the people who did it had the ability to see through the very eyes of the former humans. I don't have to tell you that some of these would be the forerunners of the Gabbers. And that Jube Gabber was hurt because he happened to be looking through the eyes of that pig man in the sinkhole when I shot him.

There was also a tribe that had snakes as their totem. This group was so antisocial and vitriolic that it was ostracized by the others and mostly died out, with Old Man Black the only practitioner who managed, apparently through sheer cussedness, to stay around.

Finally, the hyenas, which were the third

group's totems. Given the reputation of hyenas, it's odd that people from this clan would be the peacemakers, the people who tried to keep a lid on things, but that's how it turned out. These slaves were the antecedents of Ma Stean and Mrs. Davis and, yes, of Patricia, although the line may have been so diluted by the time she was born that Pat has only vestiges of those traits. Or powers.

In Africa, the totems for the pig clan were bushpigs and related animals, for the snake clan cobras and black mambas. Once in Arkansas, what those people had to work with were feral and domesticated swine, and, respectively, the local snakes, including rattlers, water moccasins, and copperheads.

The hyena clan was a little different story. As David explained it, the hyena looks like a dog but is actually more akin to a cat, so most of the hyena clan took the common felis domesticus as their totem, along with an occasional bobcat. But a few of them went with dogs. When I told David there were very few canines in Mackaville, he explained that the dog people had been driven out, but was unsure of how or why. He also said that Ma may have a little of the dog people in her, which would help explain MacWhirtle (who shares a "Mac" with the town's founder. Coincidence?).

I should also tell you that the patriarchs of these factions had the ability, so David told me, to actually slow down, if not completely retard, the aging process. David

himself was living proof, even if he'd been
kept alive by something other than his own will
and imprisoned in an animal's body. So,
according to David, are the Gabber brothers —
his half-brothers, sharing the same mother
(their father fell to his death from a catwalk
in the plant; Jefferson's mother remarried,
something that set the Gabbers against her and
David) — and Old Man Black.

Yes, John, it's damned incredible. But for
all of that, it makes sense.

When the economy of Arkansas went sour
during the Civil War, Mackaville managed to
persevere. As you may remember from Pete's
account, the patriarch was a freethinker, especially when it came to race relations. He had
at least one black wife, and some of the hand-
picked white men he brought in to run shops and
do other things in the town also intermarried
with the slaves, which had become something
more than that by the time of the Emancipation
Proclamation. (Several of those white folks,
interestingly enough, came from a nearby
Utopian community that had folded its tents.)

It was, to put it simply, a town whose
inhabitants were black and white and various
shades in between, all mixed in together right
in the middle of Dixie and the heart of a
country torn by a war over slavery, a little
universe unto itself that minded its own business and kept the packing plant ginned up,
sending out ham and chopped meat and other
canned products to the rest of the country even

as its people of different colors intermarried and had their cream-and-coffee-colored kids. (Although there were still, of course, several full Negro and full Caucasian families.) Outsiders seldom came around, and when they did, the whole town knew what to do to keep them from finding out that the population and both management and labor at the town's only industry was mostly colored or part Negro. Knowing full well the Klu Kluxers had burned places to the ground for less, they came up with elaborate ruses that made Mackaville look as though it were just another Southern town, with the obviously black people "knowing their places" and the others "passing."

The town's first real problem came right after the War between the States, when some of the remnants of Bloody Bill Anderson's Reb guerillas found their way into Mackaville. Word had gotten out among liberated slaves in the area that the town was friendly to them and their kind, so by the time these white hooligans showed up, the town was completely integrated. It didn't take long for some of the brighter ones to figure out the set-up in Mackaville, as far as coloreds and whites and mixed, and they began throwing their weight around and extorting the locals, threatening to expose the townspeople to vigilante groups if they didn't get what they wanted. It was not quite a reign of terror, but it upset the equilibrium of the town in a big way, and crimes of robbery and violence jumped.

"These were _immoral_ men," David said. "They cared nothing about God or any of his creation, only in feathering their own nests at others' expense. I was very young then, but I remember how Mama would always duck me into doorways when she saw one of them coming, and hide us both until he'd passed. I could smell the evil on them when they went by."

Right about now you might be asking yourself why the townspeople didn't just take care of these troublemakers early on. Self-defense in the form of murder was more accepted then, and it was often the easiest and best solution. Plus, the people who made up Mackaville's citizenry didn't even have to get their hands dirty; they could use their animals, just like they tried to use them on me.

So why didn't they? It's because these white ruffians were under the protection of the Gabbers. It wasn't overt, but people _knew_, just like they know things in our hometown of Hallock or any other small town. And this is where David gave me another shock, handing me an important piece of the puzzle I've been trying for weeks to dope out. The Gabbers and Black, who'd had a nervous truce for years, knew that the ex-Rebs were extorting money and robbing people around the area, and they made a deal to protect them in return for a cut of the profits. David suspects they did in one or two of them via pigs or snakes, just to get the attention of the rest.

I imagine you've figured why this part of

the story gave me such a jolt, but in case you haven't, I'll just mention that log I found in the cave. Remember? Besides the names of the Gabbers and Black, there were surnames on those pages that belonged to people I either knew about — like Postmaster Gibson — or I'd interviewed since hitting town. I now knew these were likely descendants of intermarried Rebs — and I realized there could also be more ancient souls in that group, men still standing who had been complicit in the raids on town and hill people more than 70 years ago. Like Black. Like the Gabbers. It was nuts, but in a weird way it made perfect sense.

Over the next decade or so, more and more of these ex-Johnny Rebs moved to Mackaville, until the town that had been so integrated began to pull back and become mistrustful, falling into camps and factions where before there had been a kind of harmony. This especially was true, according to David, with the all-coloreds and the all-whites, the latter group mostly composed of Anderson's bunch and the friends they'd persuaded to move in with them. Suspicion, falling along racial lines, ran through the town like a disease.

Still, an uneasy peace persisted — until that day in 1889.

It actually happened, David says, over the better part of three days, and it was precipitated by the return of several Buffalo Soldiers from years of the Indian Wars. A dozen or so of them had joined up together from Mackaville and had been mustered out together as well.

You remember your history. These men were all Negroes, and they were not only battle-hardened but also used to a community that was far different from the one they came home to. Their return was the catalyst that ignited the Cleansing.

David: "It was three days and nights of living hell, of fire and blood, and there was nothing anyone — even us preachers — could do to stop it."

The rioting began when three ex-Rebs gunned down one of the Buffalo Soldiers in a barroom. In cold blood, David said. The Gabbers and Black, given their relationship with the Rebels, at first fought on their side, as surreptitiously as possible. David, who had remained uninvited by his half-brothers to join the family business, figured out their treachery and went to them, threatening to expose them to the other side if they persisted in backing the other side. They warned him against saying anything. He did, though — feeling it his duty as a man of the cloth — and they took their anger out on both him and his family.

(Here, David choked up and went quiet, wiping at big tears as he looked away from me. It took him several minutes to compose himself enough to finish the story. While I waited, I thought about how this must've led to their somehow transforming him into the boar hog that confronted me in the mountains. If you accept that someone could do that — and Lord help me, I have — then it would follow that he would've been especially susceptible to their control because of the blood of their clan that flowed through his veins.)

David's warnings about the Gabbers were too little, too late. By the time they had murdered his wife and children and taken him hostage, they had seen which way the wind was blowing, switched to the colored side, and became passionately involved in the rout of the interlopers. And a rout it was. Even some members of the cat faction, the voice of reason in the community, entered in. David remembered a story about mountain lions attacking the whites who'd fled to the mountains. (Again, he doesn't know for certain whether the cats and snakes actually changed from human to animal and back or whether their clans were just able to manipulate beasts and see through their eyes. He thinks it possible that only the Gabbers have the power to transform others, as they did him.) David, along with a few others — including the poor bastard I shot up there in the mountains — were surreptitiously saved by the Gabbers for their own nefarious reasons and purposes. Maybe their "saving" David had something to do with his blood relationship to them; or perhaps, as was the case with the one who'd been with him in the sink hole, because of his great strength.

When the Cleansing finally subsided, not

only the guilty but many innocents had been slaughtered, with men, women, and children swept up in what became a riot over race. After it had finally cooled down and every last damned ex-Confederate murdered (along with many other whites, blacks, and in-between people, most of whom took the Negro side) the town's leaders, with the Gabbers front and center, became petrified that word would somehow leak out and state police and vigilantes would descend on the town and rip it to shreds. It wasn't just about all the killings. They knew if area vigilantes and those guys Steinbeck called "poolroom boys" in Grapes of Wrath found out about all the inter-racial marriage going around in their little town, blacks and whites working and living side by side as equals, all hell would break loose. By that time, the state's anti-miscegenation laws may have been mostly toothless, but they were still on the books, and a good excuse for the law and "deputies" to come in and clean Mackaville out. So, with the help of the town doctor, they concocted a story about a cholera epidemic, which had the dual purpose of not only explaining Mackaville's decimated population but also keeping people away, at least for a while.

That story, David said, has persisted to this day, the secret being kept for exactly 50 years. Remember how I found out that the "jubilee" was right out of Scripture: a fifty-year anniversary? Well, this year marks the jubilee of that horrific riot. The Cleansing Jubilee.

I'd be lying if I didn't tell you the weight of all this suppressed and potentially explosive information hasn't done anything to settle my nerves. But I've always heard that the hard thing is the right thing, and I know I'm going to have to just continue to do my job and get it finished and the devil take the hindmost, so the next time you hear from me I will be back in Mackaville. I don't think a prayer or two would hurt, if you're so inclined. And if you are, please pray that my seventh sense is working well enough to keep me out of the hot grease.

Your pal and faithful comrade,

Robert

July 27, 1939
   Thursday evening

Dear John,
   You know that with me the thought is father
to the deed, as the saying goes, so after I
wrote you this morning I took the trolley downtown to the depot, mailed the letters to you,
and bought my ticket, thanking God again for
the largesse of Mr. Castapolous. I'm on Saturday's early-bird special to Little Rock, with a
couple of hours before I pick up the connecting
train to Mackaville. I splurged and spent the
better part of a half-dollar on a _Weird Tales_
and a _Spider_ at the station's newsstand. I'm
hoping they'll take my mind off the apprehen-
sion I already feel at returning.
   You'll note it was only a single ticket.
David's not going back with me. I didn't really
think he would, but he eliminated all doubt
when I told him of my plans this morning and
asked if I should get him a ticket as well.
   He actually looked _abashed_ — so much so that
I grinned in spite of myself.
   "Not at this time, friend Robert," he said.
We were sitting in the living room of the
boarding house, longhair music on the radio,
Miz Evans bustling around in the kitchen. He
involuntarily glanced toward her before continuing, and then looked back to see that I'd
caught him. For a moment, he flashed a grin as
big as my own.

"Yeah," he said, speaking volumes. "I need to help her for a while. This old place need some repair work, a man's touch."

I started to say something about Miz Evans maybe needing a man's touch, too, but I held my tongue.

"She thinks I ought be spreading God's word," he added. "I believe she's right. Wouldn't take much to get a church started 'round these parts. Some storefronts close by a man could rent for almost nothing."

I nodded. "If you start one, are you going to nail that silver dollar I gave you to the altar?"

David chuckled then and fished around in the pockets of his new slacks, coming up with the coin and flipping it to me. "I think," he said, "you might need this more than I do now."

As I glanced at the cross I'd scratched across the eagle back up there in the mountains, David pulled a little crucifix on a thin chain out of the front of his shirt. "She gave it to me," he said, nodding again toward the kitchen. "A good woman, Miz Evans."

"She is," I said, rising. "And you're a good man." I stuck out my hand and he took it in his hard grip.

"You remember, now," he said. "The Gabbers are mine. Promise me."

There was nothing of the animal in the way he said it. And I promised. But then I added, "May I ask you one more thing?"

"Yes?"

"Can you tell me why the Gabbers want to kill me? Because they do. They sent that man on the train. They even sent you, or something you used to be. Why?"

He shook his head slowly. "I wish I could tell you for true. It could be revenge for your slaughter of their pigs. It could be something else. Perhaps I say 'revenge' only because I understand its awful power over humanity. As it is written, 'Vengeance is mine, saith the Lord.'" He shook his head again. "I hope He can forgive me for what I plan to do."

The way he said it discouraged my asking for any details.

"You'll return the revolver to your friend who takes care of automobiles?" he asked.

He pronounced "automobiles" funny, but I got the message and told him I would. Then Miz Evans called him from the kitchen and he was up and out.

I wasn't sure how he was going to wreak vengeance on his half-brothers the Gabbers if he stayed in St. Louis and started a church. But it was clear some of the animalistic rage had left him, and Miz Evans had a lot to do with that. So, if love trumped hate, even for a while, that was okay by me.

Since then, even while I was on the trolley and at the depot, all of this has been turning over and over in my mind without my being able to come to any real conclusions. When I got back to the boarding house, I even made a list of "safe" people in Mackaville, those I could be around without feeling that they're going to turn on me.

It's a small group. An even half-dozen.

1. Patricia
2. E.V. Castapolous
3. Ma Stean
4. Pete Barlow
5. Sheriff Meagan
6. Mrs. Davis

Sure, there are others, like Doc Chavez and Mr. Foreman at the drug store and even Diffie, even though he has connections to the plant through his pop, which means he's some way connected to the Gabbers, maybe by blood. But these are acquaintances, not friends (except for Diffie, sort of) and I really don't know how they'd react if I went to them for help. Would they even be on my side? For that matter, what about Sheriff Meagan? I can't really call him my "friend." Like he told me, he was in this town before me, and he'll be in it after I'm long gone. Maybe even he doesn't want to rock the boat against the tide of the powers-that-be.

I just don't know, and I'm running myself half-crazy from all these mental acrobatics. I did call Ma Stean while I was out today. I got three bucks' worth of quarters from the operator of the depot's newsstand, and I went through them all in the phone booth before I'd told Ma all I thought I needed to. But I did get out what had happened in the past few days (leaving out how I'd found David, and in what form), why I thought I had to leave town, and when I was returning. I even told her about the man on the train who threatened me, and I just said David "threw him off" without going into detail.

She seemed surprised I'd called, but she was pleasant enough, and then some.

"Robert," she said, "I'll spread the word and see if I can get things smoothed over 'fore you get back. Still, you'd best keep an eye out when you arrive, and don't tarry. Get yourself back here as soon as you can."

"I will, Ma," I told her, absently studying the numbers scratched into the wood of the booth above the phone and thinking the Gabber boys and Black might not be "smoothed over" so easily. "And I appreciate it."

The operator broke in then, and I had to feed another six bits into the slot.

"One thing," I said when we resumed. "There was a little effigy — a doll, I mean — in my drawer, and it's gone now. Do you have any idea what happened to it?"

I got no answer, and just when I thought the line had gone dead, she said, "I'm sorry I didn't have no more faith in you. Shoulda had more. I hope you understand."

I didn't, but I said "sure" and then told her I'd see her soon.

Her comment had disturbed me, and for a

little while my faith in her as one of my "safe" people was shaken. Had she retrieved the doll for Black? Were they in it together? Did their longtime residency in Mackaville cause them to ultimately band together against anything an outsider tried to do? It all left me with a queasy stomach to go with my whirling head, as well as a hell of a lot more questions than answers. I wasn't even sure I should keep Ma Stean on my short list. The only sure thing is that there's a lot more going on in that town than I know about.

I've just had a knock at my door, and it's Richard the writer. I told him I was finishing up a letter, so he's patiently waiting. I'm going to put these pages in an envelope and then ask him to send them to you. Seeing as how he's a mail clerk, he can just take it to work with him. Safe as milk.

So that's it. The next thing you hear from me, God willing, will be written in Mackaville, that cursed town with just a few wonderful people shining like stars in it. Even if I didn't have to get back, retrieve my notes, and finish the job the WPA sent me to do, I'd have to chance going back just to see Patricia again, to tell her that I want her to be my wife.

Your pal and faithful correspondent,
Robert

July 30, 1939
Sunday evening
Back in my own little room

Dear John,

I spent most of Friday poking around St. Louis, just sort of losing myself like a tourist. I'd always wanted to see Sportsman's Park, where both the Browns and the Cardinals play baseball, so I took the trolley down and looked it over. There was a game going on but I didn't go in. I also caught a trolley to the west part of town and went to the Cathedral Basilica. I <u>did</u> go in there. It was cool and full of candlelight and made you feel at peace and close to the Creator, just as any church is supposed to do, I guess. I sat there in a back pew for a long time, and when I left I felt better about things, even about returning to this godforsaken town.

After all that rubbernecking in St. Louis, the return train ride to Mackaville seemed long and tedious, but I had those two pulps to read and the time passed without too much pain. My seventh sense stayed quiet, which I saw as a good thing. Hell, I was almost calm, even though I drank gallons of coffee on the trip.

I got to eat in the diner this time, and staked myself (thanks to Mr. Castapolous) to the best meal they offered, which was a decent pan-fried T-bone steak with a baked potato, corn on the cob, and a very fresh green salad.

I also had a bottle of near-beer. Arkansas is more or less a "dry" state, with only a few "wet" counties where you can buy alcoholic beverages, so trains crossing the state are barred from selling even beer, substituting this non-alcoholic stuff. Still, it tasted all right, even if it did make me think of the hearty brew at Castapolous's place.

About halfway through that big T-bone I started thinking about how this could be like a convict's last meal, where he gets to eat whatever he wants before they stretch his neck with a rope. To dissuade myself from that line of thought, I remembered the conversations Richard and I had gotten into the last two nights before I left. He's a very intense kind of guy, and both times we found ourselves in some long discussions about writing and what it should be and do. Now, you know me, I've never thought much past pulps and being entertained. I guess I've had a vague idea in my mind for a while about putting pen to paper and creating some kind of a fictional yarn, but when I consider that, it doesn't go much further than thinking that breaking into the pulps like you've done would be something I could be proud of doing.

Richard is different. He says the pulps are escapist entertainment, and while he was careful not to denigrate them in front of me, it's clear that he thinks writing has a higher purpose than entertainment, which I understand. I told him I read Grapes of Wrath earlier this year and really liked Steinbeck and Dos Passos,

even though I found W. Faulkner hard to read
and couldn't quite warm up to Hemingway like I
know I should. I even brought up that book from
a couple of years ago, Their Eyes Were Watching
God, which I knew was written by a Negro woman.

He was familiar with all of them, he said,
and then he told me that as a writer, the most
important thing he could do was tell the truth.
And he said that while he liked poetry because
every word had to be important, he thought that
his future lay in fiction.

"True fiction sounds like a misnomer," he
said in that earnest manner he has. "But I
think fiction can have more truth in it than
any other form of writing."

I didn't tell him that if I wrote the truth
about what I'd been through over the past
several weeks I'd have the men with the
butterfly nets out beating the bushes for me.
Still, I have an idea about what he meant. The
way I see it, he was saying you've got to kind
of sneak the truth into what you write, especially if it's something that could get you
into trouble. As a colored man in today's
world, he ought to know.

Anyway.

We rolled into Mackaville a little after six
this evening. I walked over to Pete's Skelly
station from the depot, keeping an eye out but
relieved that my seventh sense was still
calmed. Pete was bustling around the pumps,
taking care of some hill-billy in a truck that
looked like it was held together by baling

wire, when he spotted me and waved, inclining his head toward his office. I went in, got a Coke out of the box, and sat down at his desk to wait. It didn't take long.

"Damn," he said as he came in. "Good to see you."

"Should I say it's good to be back?" I asked, standing up, shaking his hand and handing him back his revolver.

"Oh, yeah. Thanks," he said, as he took it and placed it underneath the cash register. Then, "Maybe you can say it's good. There was a big boil-up right after you left, but it seems to've simmered down some."

"I kind of felt like it had," I said, remembering the lack of apprehensiveness I'd experienced upon leaving the depot and striking out into the heart of town. "I might be whistling past the graveyard, but I feel okay about things."

"You want to hang around? I'll be closin' in a few minutes and I'll take you home in my car. Everything seems some better, like I say, but it might be best not to advertise your return by gettin' on the Indian. You can pick it up tomorrow."

"Tell you what. How about if I buy you supper at the Castapolous Cafe? One of his chicken-fried steaks sounds like the berries to me."

"Deal," he said, going outside and locking up the two pumps. We were out of there and walking toward Main Street in a jiffy.

E.V. Castapolous grinned and grabbed my hand just as soon as we set foot in the place, which was about two-thirds full of hard-working rails from the train yard who'd just gotten off their shift.

"You boys grab a table," he said expansively. "Be right with ya."

I steered Pete over to an empty spot at the rear, where the lights were dimmest. Word would get out soon enough about my return to Mackaville. I didn't see any reason to hurry it along.

I took the seat facing the door, a move that wasn't lost on Pete. "I thought you felt okay about being back," he said with a grin.

"I'm not rabbity or anything," I said. "But no sense letting my guard down."

He nodded, and Mr. Castapolous showed up with water for us. "Menus?" he asked.

"Naw," I said, "Couple of chicken-fried steaks with all the trimmings." I grinned. "There's still some of your money burning a hole in my pocket."

"You keep that money, Robert," he said. "What you brought me was worth far more." He took our drink orders — coffee for Pete, Coke for me — and while Pete looked quizzically at me after my exchange with Mr. Castapolous, he didn't ask any questions.

"Mr. Castapolous lent me some money before I left town," I explained after a moment. "I found some old artifacts in the mountains that I brought back for him."

"Artifacts, huh?" said Pete.

"Yeah." It didn't seem like it would hurt to tell him, so I added, "Old powder horns and a Colt Walker .44. Found it all in a cave." For some reason, maybe just caution, I felt it prudent to leave out the ledger book.

"Hmmm," he said. "Like to see that stuff sometime."

"I'm sure that'd be fine with Mr. Castapolous," I returned. "Right now, though, I'd like to know about what's been happening around here since I left. You said things had gotten better. What do you mean?"

Just as he opened his mouth to tell me, Mr. Castapolous materialized out of the smoky din with our food. Now, I don't think you know what a chicken-fried steak is. There aren't any places in Minnesota I know of that have 'em on the menu, although I guess there could be a few, but here in Dixie they're a regular damn staple of existence. To make one, you take a piece of steak, a cheap cut, beat it down, flour it, and then fry it like chicken — hence the name. It comes with a crust and some of the best ones are about as big as a dinner plate. The Castapolous Cafe has its own version, which is not beat so thin. Mr. Castapolous doesn't like using cheap steaks, so his don't have to be pounded with a mallet to get them tender. He fries them crispy with a thick golden crust and lots of garlic and one of them would feed a village in Abyssinia. The spicy gravy he pours over them is like icing on a cake.

While Pete and I were polishing off two fine examples of the Castapolous culinary art, Pete caught me up on the events that had followed David and my hurried exit from Mackaville.

"The Gabbers had people out lookin' for you for the first couple of days, an' I don't think they was wantin' to invite you to a lodge meetin'. They all seemed pretty disturbed about somethin'. But then on Sunday things seemed to quiet down," he said. "Dunno why, but the peace seems to be holdin'. Leastways, no one's come by lookin' for you lately."

"Good," I said. "I hope it lasts long enough for me to finish up my work here." Then I told him about my phone conversation with Ma Stean.

"I told her most of what I told you the night we left town — except for the part about David being a killer hog that attacked me before he was transformed. And I told her some stuff I found out later from David about the Gabbers, which might explain why they wanted both him and me." Pete didn't change his expression at all, even when I told him about how the Gabbers had some sort of psychic connection with the pigs, how they could look through their eyes, how they could even change people into animals. I didn't have any logical reason to stop short of talking about the 1889 riot and the Cleansing, but when I started to get to all of that something told me to pull back and keep it to myself. I did tell him about the man David threw off the train, although, as with Ma, I didn't go into the grisly details.

"I've got to think this all out before I approach the Gabbers, and I have a feeling I'll be safe enough at Ma's," I said, and I did. I could only hope that calm feeling was the seventh sense and not just some sort of hope on my part.

"I imagine you will," he said. Then, after a bite of chicken-fried steak, he continued. "You know, Robert, how crazy this all sounds?"

"To you?"

He shook his head. "Naw. I been here too long. I've heard lots of things. I ain't been shocked since I found out ice-cream cones were hollow. But if you tried to tell anyone outside Mackaville..."

"Yeah. I know."

We finished, walked back to the station, and took Pete's Hudson to Ma Stean's place, which looked great to me despite everything that had gone on there in the past few weeks. Before I even saw Ma in the doorway I heard an excited yipping and a little ball of fur shot out of the doorway and down the sidewalk toward me. As he jumped up and down at my shins I got my case out of Pete's back seat, thanked him, and headed for the front door.

Ma stood there, and she sure seemed glad to see me. She even gave me a big hug, which is something she'd never done before, and told me she had some food ready for me. Over her shoul-der, I spied all three of her boarders sitting around in the living room, listening to the radio. Dave looked up at the sound of my voice, grinned, and gave me a wave. I saluted him.

"Thanks, Ma," I said. "But I just ate and I'm kind of beat from the train ride. I've got a lot of things to write down tonight, too. So I'll just slip on upstairs, unless there's something I need to know."

"Nothin' so important it won't wait 'til tomorrow," she said. "You an' Mac go on up. I'll telephone Patricia an' tell her you're back. She made me promise."

That made me feel good. "Thanks, Ma," I said.

"And," she said, "things are better. Dunno why, but they are."

I nodded. "Good."

I'd made it halfway up the stairs, Mac at my heels, when she shouted after me.

"Oh, there is one thing," she said. "Sheriff Meagan wants to see you in his office t'morrow morning."

And here it came: the seventh sense, breaking over me like a Pacific Ocean wave.

So that's it. Writing this letter has pushed a lot of the adrenaline out of me and I feel like I can sleep now. MacWhirtle the wonder dog long ago curled up on the foot of the bed and has been snoring like a buzz saw for almost an hour. I took a break halfway through this letter and unpacked my extensive wardrobe of four, no, sorry, five changes of clothes. Everything's back where it should be

— except for my little effigy of Old Man Black.

I'll worry about that tomorrow. And I'll worry about Sheriff Meagan tomorrow, too. Right now, I'm having a spot of that nasty, powerful moonshine from a fruit jar, hoping to get relaxed enough to catch forty winks.

You'll remember I got it from the Gabbers. Would you call that irony, or what?

More tomorrow, I hope.

Your pal and faithful correspondent,

Robert

July 31, 1939
Monday evening

Dear John,

What a day. I repeat: What a day.

I got up earlier than I wanted to this morning, jolted out of a deep slumber when MacWhirtle barked me awake. I opened my eyes to see him running to the door, jumping on my bed, and jumping off again. It was barely dawn.

You can forgive me for momentarily thinking the worst. But as my head cleared I realized that his barking was urgent but not hostile, and since I had no sense of anything outside the door, I quickly concluded that all he wanted to do was pee. I pulled out one of my old CCC uniforms and the poor little tyke had to wait for me to dress, but I got him to the back door off the kitchen and let him out in the nick of time. I stood there and watched while he took a refreshing whiz and bounced back up the steps.

"Mornin', Robert," said a soft voice behind me. Ma Stean was already up, wrapped in an old housecoat, her iron-gray hair rolled into a bun and fastened with bobby pins. She nodded toward Mac. "Jes' like an alarm clock," she said with a grin.

I grinned back. I had that feeling again, the feeling that this place was home.

"I'll be back down in a little bit," I told her. "Soon as I shave and clean up a little.

What time you think the sheriff gets to his office?"

"S'pect he's there now," she said.

I nodded and started to leave, but she stopped me.

"'Fore you do that — someone's been waitin' all night fer ya." She nodded toward the living room, and I looked in to see Patricia, asleep under a quilt on Ma's living-room sofa. I don't know that she'd ever looked more beautiful to me. I was drawn to her like a moth to light.

Kneeling beside her, suddenly aware of my morning breath, I spoke her name and she stirred. Her eyes fluttered open.

"Robert," she whispered, and reached for me. We held each other, and she whispered again, her mouth beside my ear.

"Ma says you're all right. I'm so glad."

I could've asked her to marry me right then. But I didn't.

"Yeah," I whispered back. "I'm fine."

I held onto her a couple of seconds more and then pulled back, looking into eyes that were still clouded with sleep.

"Ma called me when you got in last night," she said. "I wanted to be here when you got up."

"You're a diamond."

She smiled. "A diamond?"

"A jewel. The best kind of jewel." I shrugged and she laughed a little. "That's about all I can do this time of morning."

"It's good enough," she said, still smiling.

"I'm glad," I returned. "Listen, I've got to go see the sheriff. But I'll be back. I've got something I want to talk to you about."

Her quick glance over my shoulder told me that Ma was in the room. It also told me that maybe she had an idea of what I wanted to say to her later. She nodded, and I squeezed her hand, got up, and left the room.

Even though I have the last bathroom shift in the morning, I don't generally take a bath then, preferring to scrub off all the road grime before going to bed. So I usually have to hit the tub early in the evening, because there always seems to be at least one of my fellow boarders coming in from the railroad shop wanting to do the same thing at the end of the day. Sometimes, I'll wait until about midnight to make sure everyone has had his turn. This morning, I was the first one up, so I took a spit bath, once over lightly with a hot wash cloth, and shaved. I couldn't help but think about how I'd done the same thing my very first morning in Mackaville, weeks that seemed like eons ago.

Breakfast wasn't supposed to be on the board for at least another half hour, but when I got downstairs I saw that Patricia had slathered butter on a thick slab of Ma's fresh-baked bread and poured me some coffee. I thanked her as I gobbled and drank, wanting to get my interview with Sheriff Meagan over as quickly as possible. I hadn't had a good case of the heebie-jeebies since I'd gotten back, but they were threatening every time I thought about what he might want, and I had to chalk that up to the seventh sense, because the guy had always been fair with me. As I've written you earlier, I counted him one of the good ones in town — one of the few.

The sun was just pushing itself over the mountains when I hit the road to town, wishing I'd ridden the Indian home the night before and the hell with everybody knowing I was back. It was a good stout hike to the sheriff's office, and as I walked I tried to straighten out all the things that had happened in my life over the past few weeks, to force them into line so that they could lead naturally to one another and I could then finally make some sense out of it all. But my mind refused to function that way, ranging off into other areas and refusing to be corralled.

It was going to be a hot day. Even this early, humidity hung over the town, heavy and still. No breeze, which meant that the packing-plant odor, which never really disappeared, was especially noticeable. I found myself hoping for just a little wind, not just to waft away the smell but also to stir up the humidity. I'd already started to sweat.

Sheriff Meagan's office was at City Hall, a fairly new three-story edifice built by the WPA in the square that sits right in the middle of town. Most of the other businesses in Mackav-ille are built around that square, facing inside, sidewalks running in front.

It was cool inside City Hall, a welcome respite from the outside. I seemed to be the only living soul in the place, though. Going down the directory just inside the door, I found the office. It turned out to be the first room on the right. I went in, pushing open a door with pebble-grained glass that had a big six-pointed golden star and the word "SHERIFF" painted on it. Hard to miss Meagan's baliwick.

He apparently wasn't the only one who got to work early. Despite its being not even eight o'clock, there was an older lady already sitting at a beat-up old metal desk who looked like she'd been there for hours. Hell, maybe she had.

"Hello," I said.

She gazed at me over the top of her horn-rimmed glasses, looking like a prune with eyes, and didn't say a word.

"My name's Robert Brown, and I'm here to see—"

"The sheriff is in a conference right now," she interrupted in a prim, dusty voice. "He's very busy. It may be some time before he can see you. Maybe you'd like to give me your telephone number and I can call you later and give you an appointment."

I grinned. The old bullshit brush-off.

"I came in this time of morning because he asked to see me as soon as I returned to town," I said, still smiling. "If you'll tell him Robert Brown is here, you'll save us both a lot of trouble."

I could see the struggle on her ancient face. On the one hand, she wanted to tell me to go to hell — in the most ladylike, Daughters of the Confederacy way, of course. On the other, I suspected he had already left her word of some kind about me.

"Well," she said snippily, "if you'll have a seat over there, I'll tell him you're here. But I don't think he can see you right now."

I went over and sat on the wooden bench the woman had indicated while she got up and went through the door behind her desk, holding it open enough for me to see that there really were people in with the sheriff. What's more, they were all wearing uniforms. Counting Sheriff Meagan, I spied at least three men in those khaki outfits, a couple of guys in blue I took for the local police, and what looked to be an Arkansas State Trooper, dressed in dark green. Then she pulled the door shut and I didn't see anything else.

In a few moments she was back out, giving me what I suppose passed for a smile with her.

"Sheriff Meagan would like you to wait for him," she said, her face a rictus mask. "He won't be long."

I smiled, nodded, and picked up an old _Liberty_ from the magazines stacked on a scarred table beside the bench. I'd gone through it, two _Times_ (including the controversial one with "Man of the Year" Hitler on the cover), and a _Life_ before the door finally opened and the conference members came out and paraded by me, a couple of them nodding a greeting, a couple of others staring at me as they passed. Although I'd been in Mackaville the better part of three months, maybe my old CCC outfit with the leather leggings was still unusual enough to cause them to give me the once-over. Or maybe they weren't amused by my clothing at all. Maybe they knew more than I thought they did about me.

One, a fat slob wearing a disheveled sheriff's uniform from a nearby county, seemed especially interested. He even stood in front of me for a moment, a kitchen match between his sausage lips, looking me up and down. I nodded with exaggerated politeness, and he turned away and headed for the exit.

Sheriff Meagan came out last, saying his goodbyes. He stopped in front of me as the rest of them pushed their way out the double doors.

I glanced at my strap watch. It had been 47 minutes since I'd sat my white ass down on that hard wooden bench.

The sheriff didn't even say hello. "C'm'on," he growled, nodding toward his office. Following him in, I took the chair in front of his desk and sat down as he seated himself opposite me. He looked up with narrowed eyes.

"Did I tell you to sit down?" he snapped.

I started to rise, and he waved me back.

"Aw, hell," he said. "Never mind. Siddown."

He fumbled around in his front pocket for a cigar and jammed it in his mouth, leaving me to sit and wonder just what the hell was going on.

Lighting his stogie and glancing up, he said, "You smoke?"

"If that's a rum crook, you bet I do," I told him.

He actually cracked a smile then and handed me one. I happened to have my match safe with me, so I lit up and blew out a cloud of rank smoke, matching his own exhalation. I still didn't know what was up.

Then he got right down to business. "You went hunting a week or so ago, in the mountains up north. That right?" It didn't really come out like a question.

"No, Sheriff," I said. "I did go up there, but it was to do some exploring and camping, not hunting."

"You didn't shoot anything?"

And there it came: the seventh sense. Why? Was it <u>warning</u> me about something — something about the sheriff? About what I should <u>tell</u> the sheriff? Anxiety suddenly pumped through me like runaway blood.

"Yeah. Yeah, I shot a squirrel — and some wild pigs that attacked me. But I didn't go there to hunt anything."

As I watched, his face began to redden. Very carefully — <u>too</u> carefully — he laid his cigar in a big glass ashtray atop the cluttered desk and stared hard at me.

"Don't give me that crap, Brown. There were dead pigs strewn all over the landscape."

"Like I said: I was attacked."

Suddenly, he slammed his fist down so hard

that the Crook bounced out of the ashtray onto the desk top. Grabbing it up, he pointed it at me like a gun.

"God damn it!" he shouted. "I want the God-damned truth about what you were doing up there!"

The seventh sense jerked through me like waves on a seismograph. I didn't know how much to tell him, because I didn't know how much he already knew. Hell, I didn't know how much the town knew. Maybe everyone knew about David Jefferson, and how he'd suddenly shown up with me and then how we'd gone off together. The Gabbers knew. They knew everything. How many others did?

Was it possible this meeting had been about me?

Then, I thought: If the sheriff knew about Jefferson, maybe he knew about his piggy comrade-in-arms, the one whose corpse was now rotting at the bottom of a sink hole. Sure, he'd attacked me. But still, I'd killed him, and if the law somehow came up with the corpus delecti and decided it wasn't self-defense, they could damn sure stretch my neck for it.

The way I saw it, I didn't have a lot of choice. Meagan may have been one of the lawmen who wouldn't mind watching me dance at the end of a rope, but he was the only one I knew on any sort of a personal level. Really, he was my only hope. So I decided to dump the whole bag out — omitting any mention of how I'd met and dealt with Jefferson and the beast-man who'd tried to murder me.

I told him about everything else, though: the cave, the gun, the ledger, the whole megillah. I even told him about getting the Mannlicher from Mr. Castapolous. I had the idea that my Middle Eastern friend didn't necessarily want people to know that he'd lent me the rifle, but I didn't necessarily want to wind up in the Mackaville jail either, and the red-faced explosion I'd gotten from Sheriff Meagan indicated he wouldn't mind tossing me in the hoosegow if I said something that set him off.

Funny. The more I talked, the better I felt, and I was conscious of the sheriff's face lightening up, too. The longer I went on, the more he seemed to relax. He even began puffing on his stogie again, although mine lay untouched in the ash tray.

Once I'd finished, he picked up his phone, got the operator, and in a jiffy he had Mr. Castapolous on the line. I listened while he related the story I'd just told. Then, he asked Mr. Castapolous if he could bring over the Colt Patterson I'd brought him from the cave. The sooner the better, Sheriff Meagan added.

When he hung up, he nodded toward the half-consumed Rum Crook of mine, sitting there burning to ash.

"Go ahead," he said. "Smoke it 'fore it's gone. E.V.'ll be right over." As if to show me how to do it, he inhaled deeply, blowing out the steely smoke in one steady stream, his seething demeanor gone.

I was feeling quite a bit better myself.

"Know how I knew about the pigs?" he asked.

"No, sir. I don't."

"I was up in the mountains a couple days ago, lookin' around. Spied lots of buzzards about a mile back in the hills. That's where I come onto those pigs."

"You did some damn fine shootin', I'll give you that," he added. "You're lucky, too. Those razorbacks are dangerous as hell. They've killed a lot of livestock. A few men, too."

He paused, eyeing me. "How'd you know to get up on that rock you told me about?"

"I just had a premonition," I said truthfully. "I thought something was following me, so I climbed up to get a better vantage point. Even then, one of 'em got up there with me."

"Either you're a hell of a shot, or E.V. gave you a hell of a gun," he returned. "Them pig corpses had been pretty well worked over by the buzzards and the coyotes and the other critters 'time I got there, but from what I could tell, most of their heads was blown clean off."

"It's a hell of a gun, all right," I said. "But I've always been a pretty fair shot, too."

He said, in a funny kind of tone, "Yeah. I could tell."

At that point Mr. Castapolous showed up, breathless and looking more than a little apprehensive. He relaxed, though, when the sheriff made it plain he just wanted to verify his part in my story. I got a break when he showed Sheriff Meagan that old Colt, because it was clear the sheriff was a little daffy about firearms. Both of them went into fits over that old gun I'd found in the cave, which Mr. Castapolous had cleaned up beautifully.

It also turned out that the sheriff was familiar with the Mannlicher I'd borrowed, so that issue was quickly laid to rest. It didn't take long after that for Mr. Castapolous to be dismissed, although not before Sheriff Meagan tried to buy the Colt from him. The old cafe owner gave me a big wink as he scurried out the door.

After he left, Sheriff Megan turned to me, and there was ice in his voice again. "The night after you shot the... pigs, I understand you left for St. Louis on a <u>sightseeing</u> trip." The emphasis he gave <u>sightseeing</u> told me he didn't believe that was my purpose at all. "Since you were gone, you might not know we had some hard rainstorms for three days after that. Real toad-stranglers, Brown."

"That right?" I couldn't see where he was going, but it looked as though his face was getting red again. Somewhere inside me, a voice whispered, <u>look out</u>.

Reaching inside his desk, he brought out a manila folder, opened it, and extracted an 8 x 10-inch photo.

"See if you can tell me anything about this," he said, sliding the picture toward me.

The image was so revolting that I inadvertently jerked a little. It took me a moment to realize what it was: a naked male corpse, lying on its back on the ground, arms stretched over its head, dead fingers stiff and claw-like. The picture hadn't been taken immediately after death; the parts of the body that were eaten away attested to that. Around the face, greasy strands of very long lank hair were stuck to his skin, plastered down by blood and rain, and there was a bullet hole through his neck, just below the chin, making his head lie at a strange angle.

At first I thought it was the guy who'd been with David Jefferson. But the more I looked, the more I could see it wasn't him. They were a lot alike, but this one's face was thinner, with a long pointed jaw and corvine nose.

"Ugly son-of-a-bitch, isn't he?" I said.

"Yeah. Know him?"

I pushed the photo back toward him, feeling a little sick. "No," I said.

"Found him up there about a mile away from where you slaughtered those pigs. Sure you don't know him?"

"No."

"I think you're lying, Brown." He said it conversationally, but there was hardness behind it. "In fact, I think he came at you out of the hills and you shot him."

All I could do was shake my head. What could I say? Yeah, sheriff, I shot a man up there, but this isn't him?

I knew I was still a stranger to him, and to the whole town. It takes a hell of a lot more than a couple months of residency to be accepted as one of the townsfolk — not just in Mackaville, but anywhere. I knew that. You and I, we're from a hamlet ourselves, albeit one that's hardly as sinister and crazy as this one. Now, I realized I was sitting across from a man I thought I trusted but really barely knew, one who seemed to be getting ready to charge me with murder.

I'd read somewhere, probably in a pulp, that when in doubt you should go on the attack. So I leaned across the desk and said, in as tough a voice as I could muster, "Now look, Sheriff Meagan. I've never seen that guy before. Just because you found him up where I shot those hogs doesn't mean I shot <u>him</u>. That's what you're saying, isn't it? I admit I was up there. I admit I killed some hogs. But that's a whole hell of a lot different than shooting down a human being!"

<u>Except in Mackaville</u>, I thought.

"Shooting pigs doesn't give you any grounds to accuse me of killing some crazy man running around the woods. Hell, don't you think I know the difference?"

I was standing when I finished, looking down at him. I'll admit I got pretty loud there at the end, too.

I'm not sure what I expected, but it wasn't what he said next.

"I didn't find him," he said flatly. "That

fat slob sheriff up there, Rosenberg — you saw
him coming out of our meeting. He's the one.
Managed to get off his lazy ass long enough to
go out and see what the buzzards were so
excited about. Never even made it to the place
you slaughtered those hogs. Found this goon,
hauled ass back to his office, and called me to
come up and see if I could identify the corpse.
I couldn't, but I did a little more pokin'
around on my own and found your dead hogs."

He took a deep draw on his Rum Crook.
Blowing the smoke out in a steel-colored
stream, he stared at me.

"I'd be surprised as hell if it wasn't you
shot him, Brown." He said it like we were
discussing whether or not it was going to rain
today.

"I've never seen that man before. I don't
know a thing about him." I was repeating
myself, but what else could I say? Especially
since I'd had a sudden flash of thought about
the dead guy. He'd been plugged by David
Jefferson while we were getting out of there. I
remembered him banging away with that pistol
and how he told me that he could hit a bull's-
eye at a gallop when he was with the Calvary.

The sheriff interrupted my thoughts. "Yeah.
My Aunt Sadie's ass you don't." He blew smoke
at me.

"I'll tell you just what is going to happen
now," he said, his voice as flat as the desk-
top. "Not a God-damned thing. That's what's
going to happen."

"I didn't shoot that man," I said.

"Shut up!" He slammed his fist on the desk again, even harder this time. "Shut your smart-ass mouth and listen to me!"

"Yes, sir." I swallowed hard.

"My people weren't here when this town got started, but that doesn't mean I don't know or can't guess about a few things. Whoever this loony was, he was running around nekkid up in the hills and probably asking for what he got. I think you gave it to him. Bullet took him under the chin, clipped his spine, and kept on going. That last is a damn good deal for you. Without the bullet, no one can tie you to the killing.

"Even if I could, I don't know if I would," he added. "I ain't gonna give you the reasons. But that porky son-of-a-bitch Rosenberg has been up my ass once too often. I wouldn't piss on him if he was on fire."

So chances were good that meeting had been about me — or at least about the corpse that might be tied to me. I wondered what he'd say if I told him about the matched set they could put together if they went into a cave at the bottom of a certain sinkhole.

But I didn't say a damn thing. I sat still and stayed quiet, remembering something else I'd read somewhere: Silence is safe.

"That doesn't mean I like your sorry ass any better, Pershing," he said, and I knew the reference to Black Jack Pershing was not intended as a compliment.

Dipping into his shirt pocket, he pulled a couple of things out and slapped them on top of the desk. One of them was an empty case from that Mannlicher. The other was a little ball of lead. I reached for them and he slammed that meaty fist of his down on my hand. It hurt like hell.

"First, an understanding, you little prick," he hissed, keeping my hand pinned. "That slug was in the skull of one of those razorbacks. The brass was up on that ledge where you ambushed them. I didn't find anything else."

I could've told him that was because I'd picked up all the rest of the brass. I didn't.

"You take this goddamn evidence and stick it somewhere the sun don't shine. Bury it. Toss it off a mountain. Stick it up your ass. I don't give a shit. There's already plenty of trouble in this town, and putting you on trial would mean nothing but more of it. Trouble, and publicity — two things this damn town doesn't want or need.

"So as far as I'm concerned, this investigation is over. You keep your stupid trap shut and don't go on any more so-called camping trips." He removed his big fist and stopped trying to squash my hand, which, I'm happy to say, he hadn't been able to do.

"Take that stuff and get the hell out of here," he said.

Dropping the two items in my own pocket, I stood up, plucked my cigar from the ash tray, and cleared my throat.

"Thanks for the cigar, sir," I said.

He actually dropped his hand to his gun butt then, and I thought he was going to shoot me. But then he kind of laughed — kind of.

"Go on," he said. "Get out of my sight."

I did.

The rest of the day, thank God, was tension-free. I went to Pete's, retrieved the Indian, and roared out into the hills, where I was lucky enough to get a couple of interviews, which I'll be typing up now. I'm narrowing in on the end of the assignment, and — provided I live long enough — I'll be out of here soon.

I have to tell you, John, this is another world. Hell, I was CCC, and I've been cussed at and reamed out by superiors, but this was something else. I probably even left out a few of the bad words he used on me. I don't know why he changed from the easygoing guy he was before; only thing I can figure is that he's under lots of strain and pressure himself. Still, I can't imagine having that kind of a conversation with a Minnesota law officer. As is the case with every damn thing else in Mackaville, they do things differently here.

Your pal and faithful comrade,

Robert

August 5, 1939
  Saturday morning

Dear John,

   Not much excitement the rest of Monday or all of Tuesday. But Wednesday, by damn, certainly made up for it. In spades. As a matter of fact, it's probably going to take a couple of long letters to get everything down, and then I'll have to take off through the mountains and mail 'em in Harrison. I'll explain why in a little while.

   You'll see from the date line that it's been longer than usual since I sat down at the typer and banged out a piece of correspondence to you. A couple of reasons for that. First, by my calculations I am on my last twenty or so interviews, so my letters are going to be either further between or shorter because I'm going to be working like hell to get all the reports done and blow this place. Second, I have once again been OBE, Overtaken By Events, and all my attention has been required elsewhere.

   Now that I've said all that, let me say how important it is to me to keep you posted. I'm still just not sure if I'm going to make it out of this haunted bucolic burg alive, and if I don't, these letters will give you a record of what happened to me. If nothing else, they may shine enough light on this place, especially if you decide to take them to the newspapers, to keep any other outsider from suffering the same fate.

On the other hand, if I do make it through — something I'm counting on — these letters might be something I could call upon later if I wanted to write a book. Fiction, of course. Who the hell would believe this could actually happen?

I think I wrote you that I hadn't had much in the way of "hunches" or "premonitions" since my return to Mackaville. I did carry a kind of general feeling that something big was out there and it was all going to be coming to a head soon. It wasn't just a feeling, either; it was borne out by the knowledge of everything that had happened to me since I'd been here, even though I still couldn't make sense of it all. Sometimes I caught myself wondering if I'd just dreamed the whole shooting match, the snakes and the cats and the hogs and even David Jefferson, and although I knew better I found myself wishing devoutly I had.

Then came Wednesday night.

I'd noticed something unusual upon my return: People seemed to have gotten a lot chattier with me. They didn't really talk about anything important or serious, but when I was helping Pete at the station they tended to stick around and shoot the breeze a lot more than they did before.

I mentioned this to Pete Tuesday evening while I was helping him close up.

"Well, they like to talk to you," he said.

"You're different for Mackaville." He was sitting on the edge of his battered old office desk. I'd just finished washing my hands and was drying them on a clean shop rag I'd pulled out of tomorrow's bundle.

"I wonder if the trouble I keep getting into and out of has anything to do with their eagerness to chat me up?"

He snorted and walked over to the Coke box. "You know damn well it does," he said. "Most of the people in town, even some of their relatives, ain't big on the Gabbers. And ain't nobody likes Old Man Black and them boys."

"Well, but—" I started, but he interrupted me.

"Can it. I know what you're gonna say. You're gonna say you didn't have nothing to do with Old Man Black's miseries, or with Jube Gabber's having to go to the hospital — heart problems or gunshot or whatever the hell it was that put him there, which no one really seems to know — but if you didn't, then why'd you and your friend light a shuck outta town? I know you were runnin' from 'em." He reached into the box. "What'll you have? Treat's on me."

"Give me a Cleo Cola, if you've got one." It was a bigger bottle than a Coke, and I was thirsty.

"Last one," he said, after digging around in the cold water for a couple of seconds. He opened the bottle and passed it to me, adding, "Most of the people in town depend on that packing plant and the canning operation for their living, and that means they have to depend on a Gabber or two. They got no choice in the matter. But I don't think anyone would miss one of the Gabbers if, you know, something happened."

I took a drink. "Sure seemed to be lots of people who cared about them. You said half the town came by to try to find me while I was gone."

"Yeah. But most of 'em prob'ly wanted to pat you on the back." He grinned. "My cigs are right there next to you. Butt me."

I tossed him the pack of Spuds from beside the cash register.

"Robert," he said, lighting one, "you've been here for weeks now. You've been 'round to see practic'ly every old geezer in the county, and some beyond. You're in tight with Castapolous and me. People are beginning to see that you're okay."

I thought of the interview I'd had with Sheriff Meagan back on Monday morning, which had made me wonder whether I really had any friends anywhere around me. But then I'd figured for all his cussing and bluster that he'd given me a break, and maybe that was just his way.

"I'm glad to know that, Pete," I said. "Problem is, I'm sure the Gabbers and Black aren't done with me, nor me with them. How'll people feel when something else happens?"

"You come out on top," he said, "they'll prob'ly build a statue of you in the park."

"And if I don't?"

"They'll likely give you a decent burial and go on like before."

He said it like he was kidding, but he didn't smile. Instead, he just kind of eyed me for a few seconds before adding, "Naw, you'll be all right, long as you don't do anything that gets you in trouble with the sheriff — or, worse, them sorry excuses we got for town coppers."

I thought he sounded unconvincing, but I didn't say anything. I didn't know much about the Mackaville police, although I remember thinking I'd glimpsed someone in uniform watching me fight the Black twins in front of Foreman's Drug Store without doing a damn thing about it.

Downing the last dregs of my Cleo Cola, I stuck the empty in the crate by the Coke box. "I wish I was convinced the sheriff and the cops were all I had to worry about," I told him as I opened the door. "Good night."

That was Tuesday. Nice and quiet. Then, the next day, things started hopping. After taking down a story from the old mother of Samson Lowry — a man I met at the church who's always been friendly to me — I went with him to see where he was putting in an indoor toilet. He seemed very proud of his work, showing me the foundation and the two by four frame of the little room he was adding to the back of the cozy wooden house where he and his mother lived. The place was just outside of town, nestled in the foothills, and apparently FDR's Rural Electrification Act had only recently gotten to them.

"Old lady ain't let up since we got electrified," he said, spitting a line of tobacco juice and nodding toward his new well house. "She wants that indoor plumbing afore winter sets in. Seems to me I got a lotta time, but that ain't the way she sees it." He grinned at the wrinkled female face looking at us out the kitchen window, and she gummed back a smile.

Just as I started to say something, a zing rocketed past my ear like an angry bee and a chunk of the timber I had my hand on flew up.

And like a Republic serial, that's where I'll leave it for a few hours. I'm going to switch gears now and type up a few stories for the WPA. I'm really behind in that and planning to catch up today.

Plus, I've got to admit, I kind of like to leave you hanging every once in a while — especially since, in this case, you at least know they missed me.

Your pal and potential serial-scenario writer,

Robert

August 5, 1939

Saturday mid-morning

Dear John,

I've finished four reports, taken a little walk around the house (even though it's hotter than hell's hinges), and visited some with Dave, who's downstairs reading a brand-new book by Raymond Chandler, that guy who's done some real good stories in Dime Detective and Black Mask. He says it's the best damn detective book he's ever read.

Wish I had time to relax and do a little reading myself. But there's too much to tell you, beginning with the finish of the cliffhanger I left you with this morning:

HUMAN TARGETS (STILL AGAIN)

No sooner had the bullet — that's what it was, in case you had any doubts — hit the wood than Sam Lowry and I lit out for the shelter of the house.

"Them stinkin' damn kids again," he muttered as we reached the back door and hastened in. "Wait here."

I wasn't so sure it was any "stinkin' damn kids." My seventh sense had zipped through me just about the time the lead sailed past my ear. But I didn't have long to wonder. In a twinkling Sam had popped back out with a double-barreled shotgun.

"This'll get the little bastards' attention," he said, his mother moving like a ragged

wraith in the doorway behind him. "C'm'on."
With that, we slipped out of the back door and
he slid over to the side of the house, poked
the gun around the corner, and blasted off both
barrels with a mighty noise.

He looked back at me with a semi-toothless
grin. "That oughta pepper them little morons
good. Goose shot."

I must've looked funny at him, because he
exploded into a laugh. "Hell, don't let it
bother you none. They wasn't shootin' at us,
prob'bly. They get to huntin' squirrels or
rabbits and don't pay no 'tention where they's
aimin'. I let 'em have a blast from this—" he
patted the barrel of the old gun "—an' they
'member where they are and move outta range.
Hardly ever hit one of 'em, and when I do, it
don't hurt 'em much. Just makes 'em a tad bit
more careful-like."

I looked at the chunk of lead in the board.
It appeared to be from a .22, so maybe he was
right. Still, after I said goodbye to him and
his mother and fogged it out of there, I
continued to feel some pinpricks sweeping
across my body, and they stayed with me as I
guided the big Indian through the mountains
into town. But even though part of me stayed
perpetually alert for an ambush, my thoughts
strayed to Patricia, and the question I'd told
her I was going to ask her. I'd said it right
before I left to go to the sheriff's office
that Monday morning.

But I hadn't done it. I hadn't asked her to marry me.

Hell, John, I don't know why. Part of it is because I haven't been around much, buzzing hell-for-Texas through those hills and interviewing everyone I can find, and then coming back and typing everything up. I've missed lunches and dinners at Ma's for the past couple of days and when I've been there Patricia has either been busy or not there. I've explained to her why I'm so busy, and she seems to understand.

She's not a demanding woman. She hasn't said anything except that she hopes she'll be seeing more of me soon. But I know she's got an idea what I want to say to her, and she's waiting on me to say it.

I guess I could've said it to her Wednesday evening, the last time we really had a conversation. As it turned out, though, we had other things to talk about.

It was getting pretty dark when I pulled the big Indian into the shed outside Ma's place. As I fastened the door shut, I noticed a quartet of cats staring at me from beside the fence.

Even with what I knew about this town and its animals — or maybe because of what I knew — I still felt a little uneasy around the felines, especially when they gave you that old battlefield stare. A garden-variety cat doing that is bad enough. In Mackaville, you never know exactly what extra something might be shining through those unblinking eyes.

Still, I said hello to them all, speaking calmly and quietly even as the seventh sense began churning inside me again. It continued as I walked past the animals, heading for the back door. There was a big moon rising, and Patricia was outlined against it as she stood there on the steps that led to the kitchen.

"Take me to the shed," she whispered. "Bring your motorcycle out. Pretend you're showing me something."

I nodded. Speaking in a normal tone, I said, "Hey, Pat, c'm'ere and look at this."

We walked together in the moonlight, and I opened the door, which screened us from anyone in the house. Then she was in my arms and kissing me. I held onto that as long as I could, but in a few moments, she pushed away.

"Listen, now," she said, still whispering. "I have to tell you something. I overheard Grandmother and Ma talking. They didn't know I was listening. They said the board is meeting tonight to decide about you."

I'll tell the world _that_ kicked up my anxiety a notch or two. "_What_ board?" I whispered back.

"At the plant. The Gabbers have called a meeting."

"Damn." I hissed, then: "Sorry. Didn't mean to cuss."

"You're right. It isn't a good thing. The meeting, I mean." In the moonlit night, her eyes were luminous.

"All right, Pat. Thanks. You'd better get

back in the house before Ma gets suspicious and comes out here."

"What are you going to do?" We were still both whispering.

"I think I'd better try and eavesdrop on that meeting."

Her eyes narrowed. "No," she said quickly, her voice rising. "You mustn't. If you get caught—"

I put a finger to her lips, and they trembled against it. I got the impression she was scared stiff, and I couldn't leave her in that state.

"Okay, yes, you're right," I told her. "I've got a lot of work to do anyway. You know that. I guess I'll just have to wait and see what the verdict is on me. When I find out, I'll take care of it."

She grabbed me and kissed me hard, although I wasn't sure whether it was out of passion or relief. Then I fastened the shed door and we both headed for the back door. I held her hand until we got to the steps, then I let go. I knew that Ma, and probably the boarders, knew that things had gotten serious between Patricia and me, but we both still thought it best not to flaunt it.

MacWhirtle, barking like a maniac, sped out to greet us.

Ma was stacking dishes in the big sink as I stopped to pet Mac, and she smiled at me while lightly admonishing Patricia for ducking out on her dishwashing duties.

"I wondered where you'd gone, girl. Now I know, though." She flashed another smile at me, and as Pat left me and stepped up to the sink, rolling up her sleeves, I couldn't help but wonder if Ma's down-home friendliness was a put-up job; that she was in her way just as bad, or as animalistic, as the Gabbers and Old Man Black. Sure, David had told me how the folks with the cat totems were the ones who'd kept the town together, but they had to do it with the snake people and the hog people as well, and maybe that bond between these... animal humans were stronger than the bonds they could forge with any regular person.

Like me, I thought.

"You done missed supper," Ma said. "But I know you was workin' out in th' hills an' you prob'bly need somethin' for strength. Boarders cleaned me outta gravy and mashed taters and greens, but there's still some meatloaf and bread, if you want a sandwich."

"You bet I do," I said, forcing a grin. "Thank you, Ma." The meatloaf was still sitting on the carnival-glass serving platter, and I fixed up a big sandwich, got a glass of milk, and headed to my room, skirting the living room where Mister Clark and Paul were listening to a Lowell Thomas broadcast. I would've normally been interested in joining them and getting the latest European war news, but not then. I had too many other things on my mind.

Up in my room, I munched on the sandwich and sipped at the milk while forcing myself to

start out writing the stories old Mrs. Lowry
had told me — and there were plenty of 'em.
(This is one of the reasons I didn't write you
Wednesday night. But not the only one, as
you'll see.) My windows were open, of course,
and I worked at Mrs. Lowry's remembrances for
at least an hour, until I heard Ma's car door
slam. Then, as quickly as I could, I changed
into the darkest clothes I had, which were the
black slacks I'd gotten for my dress-up dates
with Patricia plus a dark blue shirt, and
slipped on the moccasins I use for bedroom
slippers. Then, leaving my light on to hopefully fool a casual observer into thinking I
was still in, I opened the window screen, let
myself out, slid down to the edge of the roof,
eased myself down slowly, and made the eight-
foot drop. It was the second time I'd done that
in the past few weeks — the other time, you
might remember, was when the Blacks had showed
up at Ma's door one night, looking for me — and
this time it seemed even easier to fall and
roll. I hardly felt myself hit the ground.

A gibbous moon webbed the town with shadows,
and I stood beside the shed for a moment to let
my eyes adjust, hoping MacWhirtle didn't sniff
me out. He hadn't shown up at my door yet that
evening, which probably meant one of the other
boarders had lured him to the living room with
some table scraps or a bone or something. That
little dog loved me, but he loved to eat, too.

Once my eyes adjusted, I took off in an easy
jog for the packing plant, which lay in the

distance beside the rail tracks, staying near enough to the streetlights for them to guide me, but far enough away to remain undetected. That was the idea, anyway.

The plant was easy to spot because, even at this hour, it was still lit up. Either Pete or Diffie, whose dad had some sort of medium-high position there, had told me that they were working around the clock to fill European orders for canned meat. So the war that was raging half a world away was bringing prosperity to the Gabbers and the town of Mackaville.

I was fairly close when I realized that, while I'd been able to duck the occasional human and automobile that showed up in my path, I nonetheless had company. Barely visible in the shadows around the sidewalk were a couple of cats, staring at me, standing up with muscles taut as though they'd been running and were ready to run again. I didn't know how long they'd been with me, and seeing them gave me a bit of a chill, but I knew in this town you could hardly run out on cats. So I just nodded at them and kept on course.

I arrived at the plant from the west. The south side is the main entrance, and as I peered around the corner I could see the parking lot was lit up, big ballpark-style lights shining over autos parked in rows. One of those vehicles was Ma Stean's big Buick. It sat very close to the little guard house set up at the edge of the lot, and as I looked I saw the gate keeper moving around in it. Too risky for me to try to enter on that side.

Then I figured if I skirted around the back of the plant over to the east wall, where the tracks for the main train line connected with the plant's branch line, I could find a place to sneak in.

Avoiding the outside lights as best I could, I crept past at least a dozen box cars. The first two I passed were reefers, which would be loaded with ice later, at a facility beside the town's depot. I knew from conversations with my friend Dave at the boarding house that those cars were always loaded last. I kept going, passing the other cars that stretched out ahead of me, and when I got even with the bright lights of the loading ramp I crawled under the closest car and made it through to the other side, where I found myself only a few feet from the loading dock, under a metal ramp that led into the car. As I cautiously peered up, I heard a dolly thunder across the ramp above me, along with the sounds of thumping feet. I ducked back under it and listened for a few minutes as noises from inside the car indicated they were stacking boxes, and then I heard them wheeling the empty hand truck across the metal of the ramp. A little shower of sparks flashed up in front of me as a cigarette butt hit the gravel under the tracks, and the workers' gruff voices faded as they moved back into the plant.

Jumping up, I pulled myself onto the ramp and raced past the open door, glimpsing two employees as they stacked a new set of crates onto the dolly. Then, walking like I belonged there, I headed away from the area and toward the front of the building, grabbing up a clip board that conveniently sat on a desk atop the dock.

I don't know if my heart was thumping from the seventh sense or just the reality of the situation, but it didn't matter. I knew I had to be careful, but I also knew I had to brazen it out. Luckily, I didn't encounter any people as I walked from the loading dock to the plant offices on the same long concrete path. Soon, I was passing windows. The shades were drawn on most of them, panes closed in spite of the heat, but a quick peek showed me a meeting room and the profile of handlebar-moustachioed Jeb Gabber among the crowd, dressed better than I'd ever seen him dressed before. His presence was all the confirmation I needed.

There was a dark room over the office area, about ten feet above me, and I had just started wondering how I could get up there when I turned a corner and found a ladder, nailed to the side of the building. Just in case anyone was watching, I stood there a moment, looked over a pallet of wooden boxes stacked beside it (bound for Switzerland, interestingly enough), pretended to make a check mark on my clip board, and then I clambered up the ladder as casually as I could. It went all the way to the roof of the plant, but I stopped beside a window and got lucky. Because of the August temperatures, I guess, it was cracked open just a bit, the lower half pushed out from the inside. I managed to pull it open far enough for me to slide through, graceless as a hippo. At least I had the presence of mind not to land hard on the floor; the moccasins helped deaden any sound.

Even though the plant was lit up like the National Community Christmas Tree in December, it was dark as a dungeon inside the room. I stood quietly for several moments until I could gradually begin to make out shapes around me. Across the floor, near one corner, I spotted a tiny shaft of light beaming out from the flooring, and that became my destination. Slipping forward, I spread my weight across as many boards as possible to avoid loud creaks, but for all my caution, the dusty pine still gave out with the occasional tiny pop and squeak. I couldn't afford any of that. So I went down on my hands and knees and crawled, which thankfully solved the problem.

As my eyes became more and more accustomed to the gloom, I recognized what I was picking my way through: stacks of old ledgers, cardboard boxes full of papers, and odd pieces of furniture. I brushed by a pyramid of old chairs and chair parts so rickety it looked as though a sneeze would bring the entire pile crashing to the floor.

Finally, I reached the corner and looked down into the little chink of light from below, hearing a jumble of voices. Stretching carefully out on the floor, I put my ear to the crack, stirring up enough dust to trigger a good sneeze. But I caught myself in time, so we'll never know whether it would've brought those chairs thundering down around me.

Easing back against the grimy boards next to an old wooden file cabinet, the first words I heard were said in a very familiar voice: Ma Stean's.

"... going to believe anything he's written about us," she was saying. "It ain't like this hasn't come up before, some way or other, and there ain't never—"

"That ain't true!" a voice interrupted. I tried to adjust my head where I could see out of one eye and listen at the same time, but the crack was too small for me to be anything but partially successful. What I heard, though, made me think the speaker was Barney Gibson, the postmaster, whom I've been suspicious about for a long time, as you know — and not just because his surname was on the list I found back in the cave.

"Too many things have gone wrong in the last few years," he said, hostility in his voice. "Maybe the stories ain't gotten too far, but they've gotten out far enough to do us some damage. And now this — from the federal gov'ment."

"You're with the federal gov'ment, Barney," countered Ma, confirming my suspicions about the previous speaker's identity. "I get money from 'em, too. Washington, D.C. ain't the prob-

lem, and neither is Robert Brown. The only
thing that's gone wrong is Mackaville has
gotten away from us. Our children have moved
away, and they're still moving away. They ain't
coming back. What's more, there's nothing we
can do to get 'em back. What we got to do is
forget the past and adjust to the times best we
can."

A little confusion of voices erupted then,
with one emerging. It came from Jeb Gabber. I
could only see part of his body, but I remembered glimpsing him from the window. I didn't
know if brother Jube had recovered enough to be
a part of this conclave.

Jeb Gabber's voice was commanding, not at
all the hill-billy drawl he'd used when I'd
come upon him and his brother at their still.
"We ain't talkin' about them things right now,"
he said. "We'll fix that. But Brown has got to
go. He may not be postin' with Barney anymore,
but you can bet your boots he's gettin' letters
out some way or other. He's a danger to us, and
he's got to go."

"No!" That was Ma. "He didn't set out to do
anything to you Gabbers. If you hadn't tried to
kill him up there in the mountains, your brother'd be right here with us tonight, an' on his
own two feet. Now, our whole town's threatened
because of your nastiness to him. Ain't I
right?"

There actually seemed to be some muttered
agreement, which pleased the hell out of me.
But then a querulous voice I knew to be Old Man

Black's piped up, as full of venom as one of his snakes.

"Shit! I say we butcher Brown and have done with it. Not one of us is gonna do nothin' to any Gabber, but we can sure's hell get rid of that damn carpetbagger!"

John, when he said "butcher" I knew he didn't mean it metaphorically, and my blood froze. I swallowed as another man, outside my range of vision, weighed in with, "Seems to me we ought to go to this Brown and explain how the cow ate the cabbage. Way I hear it, he ain't doin' nothin' official that would draw any suspicions to us. And if we was to do anything, why, the gov'ment might step in and then we really would be in a fix."

I believe it was Ma who began speaking next, but my attention was taken elsewhere by the barely perceptible sound of stalking feet. I turned to see a huge calico cat staring me in the face with unblinking eyes. After a moment, it began licking its paw, still gazing at me, and kind of rubbed its face. Then, although its mouth didn't move at all, I— well, I heard it whisper.

"Get out," it hissed. "Quick. Black knows you're here. Snake's coming."

Yeah. It was just like that, I swear. But I didn't have any time to think about how crazy it was to hear a cat talk. Just as it whipped its head back toward the window, which I'd neglected to close, paused, and leapt for the top of the filing cabinet, I spied something —

something <u>big</u> — spilling over the open window across the room and plopping onto the floorboards.

I rose carefully to my feet and watched as the dark mass slithered its way across the floor toward me. As I said, there were stacks of paper and boxes all around the room, as well as that tower of chairs. I got behind the latter, and when that awful heavy rustling and hissing got as close as I could stand I jumped as high as I could and shoved the top of the pile hard. As it all clattered to the floor I lit out for the window, praying at least one or two of the chairs had fallen on its head hard enough to daze it, if only for a moment.

Not looking back, I made the window in about six strides, thinking each time my foot hit the floor that I'd be feeling the agony of poisoned fangs sinking into my flesh. I practically dove through that window — I'm surprised the opened pane didn't break under my weight — whipped myself around onto the ladder with one hand, and scrambled down that thing like a fireman sliding down a pole. As I hit concrete, I heard something above me and looked up to see the snake's head, shooting like an arrow out into the darkness, tongue flashing. It was the first real look I'd had at it, and it was big as a boa constrictor.

I knew the ruckus had attracted the attention of the people in the meeting, but I couldn't see any way of getting out of there without passing the windows of their meeting room. So I shot past as soundlessly as I could, my heart about to burst, pickin' 'em up and layin' 'em down, thankful that the moccasins weren't making anything but a little whipping noise as I fled down the concrete dock.

Luck was with me. There still wasn't anyone in sight nearby, and I vaulted down onto the gravel around the tracks and shinnied under the box car that had given me shelter earlier. I heard a yell then, and all hope of my getting out undetected was swallowed up in the pounding of my heart.

Feet scuffled along the dock; a lot of feet. Peering out from under the box car's other side, I glimpsed the main train line about thirty yards away. Then came two simultaneous noises: the rumble of an approaching freight train, and the sound of boots plopping onto the gravel beside the car.

Jumping up, I ran toward the main tracks, looking back over my shoulder enough to spy a knot of men moving from the blackness of the loading sheds toward me. If I could just scramble over the tracks in front of the train, then they'd be cut off. But damn! The freight had too much of a head of steam, and the locomotive roared past me well before I reached the tracks. Cut off!

It's a real bad idea to try and jump a fast-moving train, but I didn't see any other option. Still running hard, I changed my angle until I was parallel with the tracks. The box cars had been zipping by, but as I ran in line with them, they seemed to slow a little, and I leapt for the ladder on one. God almighty! It damn near ripped my arms from their sockets. As I fought to hold on, I felt my feet fly out behind me until I was waving from the box car like Old Glory. It probably only lasted a second or two, but it felt like forever and I was scared to death, thinking I was going to tumble and be ground into hamburger under those pulsing steel wheels. I had to climb three rungs of that ladder with just my hands and arms and elbows, working my way up the side of the car until one of my feet touched the bottom rung and I knew I was safe.

By the time I looked back, the packing plant was three or four blocks behind me and so was whoever had been chasing me. Ahead, the lights of the Mackaville depot were speeding toward me, so, cussing and praying at the same time, I let go and kicked away from the car with all my strength. The ground came up hard and I rolled for what seemed like a mile, the sharp edges of gravel poking me all the way down. I'll probably be picking little sharp rocks out of my hide for the next couple of weeks.

When I finally stopped rolling, I'd like to tell you that I jumped to my feet and took off, but I didn't. In fact, I had a hell of a time just making myself get vertical. I stood there, wobbly, for a long time, looking up at the steep embankment I'd just bounced down. Then I gathered myself together and made my way back to Ma's. About a block from the boarding house,

I noticed another pair of cats. The moonlight was good enough for me to see they were probably the same two cats that I'd encountered outside of the plant. No, they didn't say anything. But they sure kept an eye on me.

I slipped in through the back door, careful as a sneak thief, and got upstairs without meeting anyone. My strap watch said 11 o'clock when I made it to my room and unlocked the door. MacWhirtle, God bless him, was asleep in front of it, and for a minute I was afraid he'd start yapping and give me away. But he didn't. He just gave a little yelp of glee and greeting and followed me in.

Tired and dirty as I was, I didn't even take a bath. The hell with it. I had Mac on the bed with me and the .45 under my pillow, and I desperately needed rest. I don't even remember my head hitting the pillow. I guess if they were going to come and "butcher" me that would've been a good time, but they didn't.

At least, they haven't yet.

Your pal and faithful comrade,

Robert

August 6, 1939
   Sunday afternoon

Dear John,

   You remember that Robert Frost poem about
the boy who cut off his hand with the buzz-saw
and died? It ends something like, "Since they
were not the one dead they returned to their
affairs."
   That's how I felt when I got up Thursday
morning and found out not only that I was still
breathing, with everything in working order,
but that I had also slept like — well, I
started to say the "dead," but I'm not real
comfortable using that word again, especially
under my present circumstances. Anyway, after
finding myself in one piece, I spent that day
and the next in a kind of frenzy, gunning the
big bike through the hills and knocking down
one interview after the other. I'll tell you,
John, I was like a man possessed.
   Sure, I thought about a lot of stuff while I
was roaring wide-open over those Ozark Mountain
roads. Like Old Man Black and his sons, and how
come they hadn't been to see me again about
whether or not I was going to off their old
man. My theory was that either they'd figured
out a way to take a run-out powder to Mississippi without his knowing, or he's got the
Indian sign on 'em and they're afraid to
contact me again. A third possibility, while
remote, was that they were the ones who'd

filched my little effigy of their old man, and now they were calling the shots. I know Ma had all but told me she'd been the culprit, but maybe she'd turned it over to them. Or maybe not. I didn't mind any of those scenarios as long as it kept 'em away from me.

Then there were the Gabbers, who also had me in their sights (and probably still do). I felt like I should be a little more concerned about them, because they were powerful men in the town and I'd heard strong evidence when I'd eavesdropped on the plant meeting that they wanted me defunct so badly that they'd already tried once, with their army of swine up there in the mountains. If anything, I figured they'd be even more peeved at me now, since I'd not only not been offed by the hogs, but I'd sent a lot of them to hog heaven (or, more likely, hell) and even snatched their brother David Jefferson from their clutches.

Then again, when they'd sent those pigs after me maybe they'd been trying to get away with something. I hardly knew how the town was run, but I'd heard Jeb Gabber get called out by good old Ma at that plant meeting, and others seemed to be taking her side. So it could be that they didn't dare pull anything on me right now.

I knew they could, though, at any time. And in all this uncertainty I'd come to rely on my seventh sense, which had been blessedly silent recently. Vigilance was the key, I thought.

Vigilance, and staying attuned for any sudden premonitions.

As I maneuvered the big Indian up and down the hills, I found myself thinking about David Jefferson, wondering if I'd ever see him again, and then my thoughts wandered to Patricia. It seemed like every time I got the nerve up to ask her to marry me, something intervened. This time, Mrs. Davis has come down with some sort of bad sore throat, and of course even though she's not a kid you can't help but think scarlet fever. (I hasten to add that Dr. Chavez hasn't said that, and he's looked her over.) But Patricia is there taking care of her, and she tells me it's best if I don't come over as long as her grandma's ailing, just in case it's contagious.

So I've been interviewing by day, transcribing by night, and working at Pete's for a few hours in between. Hell, I haven't even had any time to dig into my nice big stack of unread pulps I snagged in Harrison. There were so many reports to write — all of them pretty prosaic, unfortunately — that I was still catching up Saturday when I took the break and wrote you. I may have said something about all the work I was doing in that letter.

I knew everything was going too well to last for very long, and maybe that's why I was hustling so hard to complete my quota of stories and get to the point where I could say adios to Mackaville — hopefully with Pat by my side. But sure enough, only a couple of hours after I wrote you, the tide turned.

I'd been working on the last of the backwoods tales and so deep into it that it took me a minute to notice that a little summer rainstorm had started. It wasn't much, but the drops were coming in my window, and I had to get up and shut it. When I did, I realized that maybe I'd been concentrating so much on my transcribing because I was trying to block out that familiar feeling of impending trouble. Now that I was away from the typer, that very thing washed through me like a needle-pointed wave.

Then there was a knock on my door.

That was curious. Ma and the other boarders generally know to leave me alone when they hear my typewriter clacking; maybe whoever it was had been waiting out there until the sound subsided.

I stood still for a moment, checking myself for any internal warning signals. There weren't any. So I opened my door.

It was Ma Stean.

"Sorry to bother you, Robert," she said, "but was you expectin' a package?" She called it a "pagage."

"No," I said. "Why?"

"One come for you. Got it downstairs."

The old seventh sense was ringing like a fire alarm by this time, but I kept my composure. I didn't think it was warning me about Ma, because I hadn't had that reaction to her before, even after I'd heard her speak at the

plant meeting and realized she was one of,
well, _them_, the town mucky-mucks. Since then,
I'd seen a look or two in her eye that told me
she knew I'd been there and heard at least part
of what they'd said — and what she'd said in my
defense — but she hadn't come right out with
any reference to that evening, and I'd followed
her lead, figuring maybe it was best to keep
things that way, at least for a while.

I followed her ample form down the stairs to
the front room and on into the dining area,
where a box sat on the table. No one else was
around.

"It was on the front porch," she said.
"Don't know how long it's been there, but it
musta been put there before the shower, because
the ink's runnin' on the name where the rain
hit it."

I peered at the runny letters that had
formed "BROWN." That was it. No other name or
address anywhere. Otherwise, it was a normal-
looking cardboard box, tied with cord, about a
foot square. No stamps. As I reached to heft
it, I saw that a few tiny holes like pockmarks
dotted the top and sides, of a size and ragged
shape that indicated they were made by an
icepick or a small knife blade.

The bells were really going off in my head
now. I picked it up; it was not light but it
wasn't heavy enough to be books.

Maybe it was the holes, or maybe it was
something else, that preternatural something
that had saved me more than once in this incon-

ceivable town. Whatever the reason, it hit me like a falling piano. "Oh, hell—sorry, Ma. Old Man Black sent this."

And at that moment, whatever was inside the package rustled.

Ma took an involuntary step back. "Then there's—"

"Yeah," I interrupted. "A snake. In the box. I'll take care of it." I started to add because I'm getting damn good at it by now, but I didn't. Instead, I silently picked it up and carried it out onto the back porch and down the steps. I guess MacWhirtle had been dozing somewhere in the house and heard my voice, because all of a sudden he came charging around the corner. But his happy bark turned silent when he saw me and the box, and a growl escaped his lips as he slid to a halt.

"Better keep Mac inside," I told Ma. Then, to Mac, "Sorry, old partner. I'll be back before you know it."

"You be careful," Ma cautioned. "You might not live through another bite."

When I heard the screen door latch behind me, I felt suddenly not only fearful but terribly alone. I was halfway to the shed and the sidecar of the Indian when I realized I'd taken all my weaponry to my room, feeling it best under the present circumstances to keep it near to me at night. I hadn't even stuck my little skinning knife down into my boot, where I usually kept it. So I sat the box down on the ground and turned around, intending to head back into the house — and nearly ran into Ma. I had been so intent on the package and its contents I hadn't realized that she'd followed me.

There was a hard glint in her eye, but I had the feeling it wasn't directed toward me.

"What you doin'?" she asked.

"I forgot that my knife was in my room," I said.

"'Member that big ol' bolo out in the shed?" she asked. "The one my husband brought back from the Filipino war? That do it?"

I instantly recalled the knife. I'd seen Ma use it to cut weeds and even hack at shrubs.

"It should," I told her.

"You wait then. Keep an eye out."

She headed out to the shed and I stood over the box. Maybe I imagined I saw it shake. Maybe it wasn't my imagination. The sound of MacWhirtle's barking from inside the locked door seemed very far away.

In a moment, she was back with a wooden-handled, big-bladed implement. I hefted it, nodded, and pushed the package over onto its side, the top facing away from us. Something shifted inside it.

"You might want to get back in the house," I said.

"You might need me to take the bolo if'n you miss," she replied calmly.

I couldn't argue that point. My mouth felt too dry to discuss it anyway.

Taking a deep breath, I cut one set of cords

and then the other, suddenly wondering why I
hadn't heard any rattling. If it was a
rattlesnake, his tail ought to be going to town
right about now.

The strings were so tight they separated
with a pop like a lady finger firecracker — and
that snake fired out of the box like one of
those cloth-covered springs jumping out of a
gag peanut-brittle can. I hit the ground at
full stretch and slammed the blade of that
machete-looking knife down as hard as I could.
Cut in two, the bastard began twisting, and I
diced him into writhing pieces, his blood spat-
tering the barely-green grass of Ma's backyard.
It was a few moments before the words coming
from behind me pierced through my red rage.
They were cuss words, of the kind and quality
that Sheriff Meagan had leveled against me.

I looked up to see Ma's face, beet-red, as
she spat out some epithets my old man would've
blushed at. She looked so full of fury that it
was frightening. Then, taking a deep breath,
she seemed to see me for the first time.

"That worthless miserable old son-of-a-bitch
was warned," she said, her words coming slowly
and forcefully, and not exactly to me. "I
didn't want any more of that in my house, and
he knew it. He dares to do it anyway. I
could've opened that box. Any of my other
boarders could have. Patricia, if she'd been
here." She swallowed. "He wants a fight. He's
damn sure gonna get one. Sorry bastard."

I realized then that I had never heard her

say so much as damn before. Her speech was so clean I always felt I had to apologize when I let even a mild epithet leak out. And now, here she was, scorching the air like a stevedore. Abruptly, she wheeled around and headed for the back door. I watched her march up the steps, let MacWhirtle out, and slam the screen door almost before he crossed the sill. That was one enraged old woman.

Mac ran to me as I sat in the grass, stopping and splitting his gaze between me and the remains of the snake. After a couple of moments, he stepped out and delicately sniffed at one of the bloody chunks, then turned and tried to push himself under my hand, eyes wide. Clearly, he was looking for reassurance, so I gave it to him, stroking his back and scratching him behind the ears until he lay down beside me, contented. We sat like that for a little while, the seventh sense shimmering away into the dog-day afternoon, and it took me a little time to realize that this indeed had been no rattler. It was a copperhead with a body nearly as thick as my wrist. There aren't any where we come from, but I'd been warned about them and told what they look like by the locals, and I was sure I was gazing on the remains of one. Poisonous as hell, they tell me, and the mouth, gaping open in death, showed me two wet, razored fangs.

I got up, rinsed off the blade at the pump beside the flower bed, and returned to the shed, hanging the weapon back on its hook. I got a shovel from there and went about picking up the remains of the reptile, which I dumped in Ma's burn barrel. I wanted that thing, even in pieces, eradicated from the earth, so I headed for the house where I figured to get some old newspaper and set the whole bloody mess afire. And while I was in there, I'd empty Ma's trash cans and save her a little trouble.

Well, that's what I thought I'd do. But when I slipped into the back door she was on the phone.

I heard her say brusquely, "Nora? This is Clara," before she wheeled around and saw MacWhirtle and me. "Robert," she said. "This here conversation ain't for your ears."

I nodded and quickly backed out the door, grabbing up a thick stack of newspaper pages from the kitchen table. I hoped she was through with them.

Now John, I'm not sure this next thing happened. Maybe I just thought it did. But I've learned there isn't anything crazy enough not to happen in this town.

As Mac and I approached the old oil drum Ma uses to burn trash, I swear I saw something pop up over the barrel's rim just for a second, something gold-colored and arrowhead-shaped — something that looked exactly like the head of a snake. Maybe that wasn't it at all. It could've been a trick of the midsummer light. But I wasn't taking any chances. I got out my match safe and set the corner of the newspaper pages on fire. Luckily, there wasn't much wind, and it didn't take long for them to blaze up. Then I stepped to the barrel and chucked the papers in, a shower of gray ashes and smoky sparks erupting. Within moments, a good crackling fire had taken hold.

Again, John, I'm not saying that the snake somehow put itself back together and tried to climb out of the barrel before I could get it burned up, or that somehow the head stayed alive and was making one hopeless stab at freedom. But if either of those things did happen, then I made damn sure that they wouldn't happen again, unless that damned Old Man Black was Ezekiel and he got the Lord to bring some dry snake bones back to life.

There's more, and you may get it in this same envelope. But right now I'm going to take a little walk with MacWhirtle. It's still plenty hot and humid here, and I feel like I'm writing this from inside a greenhouse. A little fresh air, preferably without the smell of the Gabbers' packing plant and the sight of poisonous vipers, may be just what the doctor ordered.

Your pal and faithful correspondent,
Robert

August 6, 1939
    Sunday evening

Dear John,

    Well, Mac and I strolled around for about 15
minutes, walking in the dusk that falls like
the Spider's cape over us and the mountains,
and I feel considerably better and more ready
to give you part two of this opus now.

    It happened earlier today. Last night, after
all that business with the snake-in-the-box, I
got it in my head to go to Mr. Castapolous's
place for a chicken-fried steak. (I think I
told you that Ma doesn't officially serve meals
on the weekends, although she makes sure you
can always get yourself something out of the
icebox if you ask her nicely.) I got as far as
the shed before I realized I just wasn't
hungry. So I went to bed without dinner and
woke up to the smell of frying bacon.

    Ma, you'll remember, makes breakfast for any
boarder on Sundays, providing that the man goes
to church with her in return. It may be that
she's bribing for the Lord, but it worked for
her and Him this morning. I jumped out of bed,
took a spit bath, and donned my best shirt,
tie, pants, and sports jacket. I've been to
church before in my CCC duds, but those seem a
little threadbare now for Sunday mornings.

    Anyway, it was a good breakfast and a good
service — I like the fact that the Reverend
Venable is calm and quiet in the pulpit, and

that he's an FDR man, too, although he tries
not to let much of that spill over into his
sermons — and after church Ma Stein and a
couple of her old-lady friends, Mrs. Cole and
Mrs. Dunlap, got into her car with us. I was
driving, but when we got to the boarding house,
they let me out, Ma took the wheel, and off
they went. There seemed to be some unspoken
conspiracy among them.

For some reason, I felt restless. Not scared
or apprehensive, just restless. (By that I mean
no seventh sense.) I couldn't see Patricia and
Pete was closed on Sundays, and I wasn't sure I
wanted to talk to anyone anyway, which is why I
decided not to visit Mr. Castapolous either. I
had those unread pulps up in my room, but I
kind of wanted to just get away for a little
while. So I decided to take in a movie at the
old Maribel Theatre, Mackaville's second-string
picture house, which offered a matinee every
Sunday for a quarter.

As usual, it was a double bill, and as
usual, they were two cheapies: I Demand
Payment, a kind of romance about the loan-shark
business, which went by quick as a wink. I
didn't check my strap watch, but I bet it ran
less than an hour. It was ok, though, and had a
couple of guys in it we've seen before — "Big
Boy" Williams and that gangster-looking gazabo
Jack La Rue.

The creative minds at Maribel (actually,
it's just one mind, that of Old Man Bell, the
owner, who's 85 if he's a day) paired this one

up with a Tex Ritter oater from Monogram called
Rollin' Westward. Neither one was any great
shakes, but they were pleasant enough time-
wasters and gave me whatever escape it was I'd
been craving.

With the newsreel (more bad tidings out of
Europe), Betty Boop cartoon, and an Andy Clyde
comedy short subject, I didn't get out of the
theater until around 5:30. The wind was getting
up then, and it looked like rain, so I hurried
on home, figuring to catch the 6 p.m. Jack
Benny broadcast on Ma's radio.

I forgot all about Jack and the gang,
though, because Pat was waiting for me beside
the shed when I pulled up on the bike, sitting
at the wheel of that old Chevy roadster. I
pulled up next to her, killed the engine, and
started to dismount.

"Don't get close to me, Robert," she said.
"We still don't know what grandmother's got,
and I may be a carrier. Just stay right there."

There was something in her tone, and in her
eyes, that disturbed me.

"What is it, Pat?"

"Something is going to happen," she said. "I
don't know what. But something's brewing."

I was willing to risk everything including
the bubonic plague to go to her and hold her,
but I stayed where I was, sitting on the big
Indian. The wind had started to whip
around us.

"Grandmother had me take the car and come
over here. I honked and honked and only raised

Mister Clark. He said you were gone. That was hours ago."

There was no accusation in her voice, but it made me feel crummy anyway.

"I was at the Maribel," I said. "I'm sorry. You mean you've been sitting here all this time?"

"It's okay. I have a message for you from Grandmother. She says it's very important that you get it and understand it."

"All right. Shoot."

She took a deep breath and then blurted it out. "From now on, you are not to go anywhere without taking a cat with you."

I was dumbfounded. "What?"

"That's her message."

"Did she happen to tell you how I'm supposed to do that when I'm driving this motorcycle everywhere I go? I don't know much about cats, but I don't see them as willing touring companions, especially on a motorcycle."

As the first few drops of wind-driven rain began to hit my face, she said, "Grandmother was very clear about this. One of the cats should always accompany you on your travels. She said to tell you it would ride in your sidecar and you should have some old clothes or something stuffed in there, something soft, to help absorb the shock of the ride and make it easier on your passenger."

As you might imagine, I had a few questions. But before I could get the first one out — as I recall, I wanted to know how I was to choose

the feline I was supposed to carry with me —
Patricia went on.

"This is very important," she told me, now
raising her voice to be heard above the wind.
"As sick as she is, Grandmother had visitors
today — Ma, Mrs. Cole, and Mrs. Dunlap. They
all wore masks on their faces, the kind
doctors and nurses wear in hospitals. Grandmother had asked me to leave the house for ten
minutes, while the four of them talked, but as
I passed by our bay window I couldn't help but
peek in at them. They were sitting around the
dinner table, holding hands, their eyes
closed. Grandmother had spread this white
table cloth out over the table, and there was
a big star drawn on it, with candles at each
point."

"Was it five- or six-pointed?" I asked
quickly.

"Five."

"Did it have the crossed lines on it that
you usually see when someone draws a star
freehand?"

She hesitated a moment. "Yes. I think so.
How did you know about that?"

There, as the raindrops intensified and the
wind danced, I remembered what I knew from my
magic studies and tried to determine how much I
could share. I wasn't sure how much she knew
about the forces in this town — she was only a
teenager, for Pete's sake — and I didn't want
to scare her. On the other hand, she was
already deep into all this, just by virtue of

being Mrs. Davis's granddaughter — and my girlfriend.

So I decided to level.

"It was a pentagram, Pat. Did it have a circle around it?"

"It did. How did you—"

"It's a magic symbol, the pentagram. It's used by good people to protect good people."

I hoped like hell it was, in this instance, good people.

Then the sky broke open and rain began thundering down. She rolled up her window and, with a wave, took off. I quickly wheeled the bike into the shed and stood there for a moment, listening as the drops splattered themselves against the metal. Then, I began to feel the presence of something. Looking slowly around in the gathering dusk, I noticed two cats sitting quietly under an ancient workbench, staring at me. I stared back, half expecting them to talk, like the one that had warned me in the attic of the packing plant.

Instead, they just stared. I don't think they even blinked.

It was as though the two cats and I were frozen there, suspended in time, looking at one another as the rain pelted down outside. If I expected some great cosmic insight, I didn't get one. It was just me and a couple of cats, having a staring contest. But it must've gone on a long time, because the next thing I knew the rain and wind had slowed dramatically and it was time for me to make a run to the house.

Ma Stean has just pulled up in her car. I guess I've been here 45 minutes or so, getting this letter typed, and I think I'm done for now.

Before my trip to St. Louis, I'd shown an interest in a copy of <u>Lost Horizon</u> on Ma's bookshelf. She told me some boarder had left it behind and I was welcome to take it and read it. I haven't cracked the covers before tonight. But I liked the movie a lot — did we see it together? — and to tell you the truth I wouldn't mind spending a little time in Shangri-La right now. So it's no to pulps and yes to James Hilton's Tibetan paradise, at least for tonight. Maybe I'll see you there.

Your pal and faithful comrade,

Robert

August 8, 1939
   Tuesday night

Dear John,

   After getting all that work done last week,
it was disappointing to have Monday turn out to
be nothing but a trip for biscuits. I rode the
Indian damn near fifty miles up in the hills to
see an old man, only to find out from his
family that he'd died last week. Since there
was nobody left in his house over 40 and no
other possibilities for me within several
miles, according to my list, I said the hell
with it and motored back in. Between notching
up my work and the other stuff that's gone on,
I feel like I've been shortchanging Pete at the
station, so I worked with him most of the
afternoon until he closed. Diffie showed up for
a couple of hours, and we all had a pretty good
time kidding around and taking care of
customers.

   There was one thing yesterday I should tell
you about. Just after breakfast, with all three
of the other boarders there for a change, Ma
took me aside. We'd all been talking about
Uncle Adolf's Nazis, how far they're going to
go and how long before FDR overrules the
Neutrality Act and America takes sides in a
real way. The discussion broke up when Mister
Clark and old Tall Paul had to get to work —
these rails are always getting their shifts
jiggered — and Dave headed for his room.

Ma waited until he'd gotten all the way up the stairs and then she motioned me to join her in the kitchen.

"Take a seat, Robert," she said, and I sat down in one of the chairs next to her wood-block kitchen table.

"I know you heard some of what was said at the board meeting Wednesday," she began, "and while I don't blame you a bit for listenin' in, I want you to understand that even though you've got that seventh sense and I've seen it work, there's a lot you don't know 'bout how this town's run. 'Nother cuppa coffee?"

"Sure." I said. She poured some thick brew out of the percolator before continuing.

"I've wondered how best to tell you this, or whether to tell you a'tall," she said, sighing. "But after you got that package, I figgered if you didn't know a few things, you might walk right into somethin'. So here we are."

I nodded.

"First thing you need to know is after you got away Wednesday night and everything settled back down, the board vote was split on you. Four to four was the final, with Mr. Otis McDermott abstaining. Know 'im?"

"Can't say that I do. I think I've heard the name, though." I took a sip of coffee. It had the consistency of warm maple syrup.

"He's the history teacher at the high school. And he knows _you_. He's seen enough of you, anyhow, to say that he thinks you're okey-dokey but that you still need to be watched."

I wasn't even sure what this hung jury was
all about, although I had an idea. They were
voting on whether or not to get rid of me.
Officially.

"Like I say, I guess it's time for you to
know a few things, and I hope to the good Lord
that I'm doing the right thing," she said,
taking a sip from her own big earthenware
coffee cup. I could see she was struggling, so
I didn't speak. It was a few moments before she
began her story, but once she began, she didn't
stop.

"Something happened here a long, long time
ago, way 'fore Bill and me moved here."

I started to say, I know. The cleansing.
David Jefferson told me.

Something, though, told me to hold back and
just let her talk.

"I'm tellin' ya, it was plenty ugly. Plenty.
We came here just after the big war, because—
well, we had us some connections in town, and
they'd wrote us about it. But they hadn't told
us that they was writin' as much as anything to
get more people in, because they'd lost a lot
of folks in that ugliness. They was needin'
more young couples that they thought could be
trusted. Miz Davis was the main one who got us
thinkin' about Mackaville, but there was
others.

"Ever'thing went along all right for some
years. Bill and I bought this place and started
rentin' out rooms, and he started up a nice
little general-notions store just off th' town

square. Did good 'til the Depression hit in '29."

Smiling a little, she sipped again at her coffee. "We had us a secret, though. We'd been buyin' war bonds fer years, 'specially durin' the good times, so we'd have somethin' for our old age. I 'spect we had about thirty thousand dollars' worth when th' crash came, and all of a sudden we had some choices to make: We could keep right on a-sittin' on it and keep it for what they call the golden years. We could cash in and live on it until things got better. We could use the money to prop up Bill's store. Or we could take it and invest in the packing plant, which was about to go under 'cause of the Depression. We chewed on it for weeks afore we finally decided to put it into th' plant. Bill was only one man, with one old fella and a couple of part-time kids helpin' him. The plant was Mackaville. It gave steady work to several hundred folks, and if it went bankrupt there wouldn't be no town left.

"Our people, Miz Davis and some of the others, had some influence on our decision, but it was ours to make. So we did. It wasn't like we cottoned at all to the Gabbers, who owned most of th' stock, but we knew if the plant kept on then the people in this town would have at least a fightin' chance to survive th' hardships bein' thrown at 'em."

She shrugged. "I sometimes look back at what we decided. Our money did help keep the plant runnin' and got Bill a seat on the board. And

with this boardin' house and our income as
shareholders in the plant, plus Bill's pension
from the U.S.-Philippine War, we did all right.
But without his little store, Bill didn't have
a whole lot to do. I think that's why he died
afore his time."

"I'm sorry, Ma," I said.

"Long time ago," she returned. "But what I'm
tryin' to tell you is: Amongst us and Miz Davis
and a few other of us, we got a pretty big
votin' block on that board. And why I'm even
bringin' it up is 'cause your safety, and maybe
even ours, depends on your actions.

"Maybe you already know that. I know about
them pigs up in the hills that you had to
shoot, and a smart fella like you's gotta know
they got somethin' to do with th' Gabbers. And
then that old fool Black—which reminds me..."

She'd been standing by the sink all this
time, her coffee cup on the drain board.
Reaching under it, she opened a drawer and
held something up. It was the wax effigy of
Old Man Black that had gone missing from my
room!

In answer to my unspoken question, she said,
"Yeah, I took it. I'm sorry. It don't mean I
like Black better'n you or anything like that;
it's more about th' workin's of this town. As
sorry as he is, he's one of us and, well, you
ain't. No offense."

"Sure," I said. "None taken." I wish I'd
felt that way.

She nodded. "Anyway, far as I'm concerned,

he screwed th' pooch — 'scuse me, Robert — when he sicced that snake on you yesterday."

It was hard to keep from laughing at Ma's vulgar euphemism, but I managed. She was so damned dead serious that a chuckle might've dynamited the conversation.

Somberly, she handed me the crude little doll. "Far as we're concerned, you can do whatever you want with it. He done crossed th' line."

I took it. "Thanks, Ma. And you're right. I don't claim to know everything I need to know to survive in this town, but I thank you for giving me some insight. It may be the wrong thing to say, but I'll do my best to protect you — all of you."

As I think I've written you, Ma's not a very demonstrative woman — most of the old ladies around here give handshakes instead of hugs — but she reached over and gave me a good one then.

"Just be careful, Robert," she said. "Be real careful who you talk to, especially when you talk 'bout somethin' other than your job."

"I will, Ma," I said. "And thanks again."

I was on fire to know more, to fit, after a damn long time, a few more pieces of this Mackaville puzzle together, but I knew for now our conversation was over, so I excused myself and headed for my room. But then I stopped.

"Ma," I asked, "may I borrow one of your hat pins?"

She leaned against the door frame of the kitchen and gave me the eye.

"I guess you know what you're doin', Robert."

"Yes, ma'am."

"All right, then. Look in the closet, second shelf. But you be careful."

Ma had her Sunday hat in a basket, and I opened it and found what I needed.

"Thanks again, Ma," I said, and went to my room, where I put the effigy of Black back in the drawer, but not before inserting the hat pin right in the middle of its chest. When Ma had taken the doll, she'd taken the pin, too. In fact, the pin I had now might've been the same one I'd used before.

Send another snake after me, will you, you old bastard? I thought as I twisted the pin a little. Then I pulled it out, exhilarated and, truth to tell, maybe a little ashamed of how much I'd enjoyed doing it.

After that, I went on out to the shed and fired up the bike, and you know the rest. I struck out with Old Man Shaver, who had the audacity to die before I could get to him.

Sorry. You don't know all the rest. I did strike out, but I also learned that it was going to be easier than I thought to carry a cat with me on my travels, as Mrs. Davis, through Patricia, had insisted I do. After the pow wow with Ma, I went to the shed to find a little calico sitting atop the stuff in my sidecar as though she belonged there. I figured surely she'd jump off once I revved up the bike, but she hung right in there and kind of nestled down into my folded-up groundsheet and rain jacket as I took off. John, just when I thought I've seen everything this crazy place has in it, something else comes along to astound me. This time, it was this little cat, fragile-seeming, that not only showed no fear but almost seemed to smile at me from the sidecar as we roared along. I've never seen anything like it. But then, I could say that about many things in Mackaville, couldn't I?

Today was a much better day for doing my job. Late last night a pretty good toad-strangler passed through with lots of lightning and thunder and hard rain, so the mountain roads were slick and muddy, the bar ditches full of running water that could've spelled disaster if I'd slid into one. Luckily, it wasn't my first time on most of those roads so I knew their twists and turns fairly well. The Simmons, names on my ever-shrinking WPA-sanctioned list, turned out to be two gregarious old people who welcomed me and spent a couple of hours trying to outdo each other with stories about their respective ancestors. I got 8 or 10 pretty good yarns, and they even fed me corn pone and beans for lunch — or "dinner," as they call it here. A couple of hours later, I had enough gas to propel me to Tulsa and back. On balance, the meal was worth it, but maybe I ought to start carrying a few Bragg's Charcoal Biscuits just in case I get asked to a bean dinner again.

I did get a pretty good scare this afternoon on my way back home. Ever since I returned from St. Louis, I've tried to take a route back to Mackaville that's different from the one I took going out. So, for instance, if there's a county line road I can drop over a mile and take, then I'll do it. (All it means is I have to consult my map either that morning or before I leave after an interview.) My theory is that if anyone gets it in his head to ambush me, it'll be harder to set up when I'm returning a different way.

I found out, however, that as theories go, this one's far from perfect.

The little calico, whom I've taken to calling Rennsdale (from Tarkington's Penrod, but you know that), seemed to be enjoying the ride back, her little head peering out from under the tarp in the sidecar every time we slowed and swerved to avoid tree trash the storm had blown onto the road.

It was a cloudy afternoon, hot and oppressive, and I'd topped a rise and was picking up speed, heading for a bridge at the bottom of the hill. Rennsdale had dropped down and curled up, as I'd found her doing every time I got past a certain speed. I imagine she doesn't care for that much wind in her face. Maybe she's just being smart, as she's small enough for the wind to pick her up and blow her right out of the sidecar if I got going fast enough.

I'd been on that road before, and I knew the bridge was very primitive and unstable, set up on piers and just about wide enough for a wagon or one of Henry Ford's old Model Ts. I'm not sure a modern '30s car could drive through it without scraping its sides on the warped old wood and metal. Every time I encountered it, I preferred to run across it with a little speed, mostly because it swayed and shook under the weight of the Indian, and it was a long way — 50, maybe 60, feet — from one end to the other.

So I hit it at a pretty good clip, and as I looked down I saw that the creek beneath was up and raging. Then, as I gunned the bike on, trying to ignore the swaying beneath me, I saw that a small uprooted tree had slid down from the side of the hill and lodged just in front of the other end of the bridge. This happened sometimes after rainstorms; whole roads could be blocked by trees and rocks loosened and separated from the drenched earth of a mountain's side.

I slowed the bike, noticing Rennsdale's little head popping up with the change in velocity. It wasn't until I had it stopped that I noticed the wind, blowing in hard gusts from the east and causing the bridge to seem even more unstable.

Keeping the big Indian running in neutral, I pulled it up on the kick stand, dismounted, and walked forward, toward the obstruction. I figured I had enough strength to pick up the top, lighter end, which faced me, and leverage the whole thing off into the roiling creek below. I don't mind telling you the swaying of the bridge made me a little queasy; I guess I could never be a sailor.

About 20 feet from the bike, I stopped. All of a sudden, the hairs on the back of my neck stood up — and at that very moment the hideous tusked face of a razorback pushed through the leaves of that fallen tree and faced me, snorting.

Things froze in time then. I knew I couldn't make it back to the cycle — and my sawed-off shotgun — before the thing overtook me. I sure as hell didn't want to jump off the bridge, because the creek was bank to bank with brown water, raging and swirling downstream, which wouldn't have given me much if any chance to swim my way to shore. Then I thought that if I'd back up really slowly I might be able to reach the bike and my weapon before the hog could get to me.

So I took a step back. The beast shook its head from side to side, slinging spittle that gleamed on its twisted tusks, and stepped forward, out of the brush, diamond-hard red eyes fixed on me. Suddenly, his gaze shifted, and I saw out of the corner of my own eye that Rennsdale had dropped down out of the sidecar and stood on the wobbling bridge with me, maybe four feet to my left. Her movement had managed to get the pig's attention, so I tried another careful slow step backward.

Instantly, the razorback's eyes were on me again. I sized him up. He wasn't as big as some of the hogs I'd encountered up in the hills, but he'd go at least a hundred pounds, and I knew that once he came for me one of us would die. As I'd found out, there's no getting away from a boar when you're on foot. You either climb a tree and prepare to stay there until help comes, or you kill it. Those are your choices. Stand and try to fight with no weapon, and he'll cut your legs out from under you and then gut you with those tusks.

With an explosive grunt, loud above the roar of the creek, my adversary suddenly charged. Reaching down to my boot, I jerked my little skinning knife out, knowing it was a futile gesture, and waited for the impact. I could only hope he wouldn't rip my legs out from under me and tumble me into that roaring brown water.

He wasn't ten feet from me when something flashed behind the charging hog, throwing itself onto to the hog's ridged back. With a tremendous scream of agony the pig jerked upward on its hind legs and tumbled over backward. Wildly, he tried to right himself, and that something — a yellow-tan ball — affixed itself to his head, yowling like a cop-car siren. Then, just like that, it was gone, and I got a glimpse of bloody empty eye sockets before the maddened pig stumbled off the bridge and plunged into the dark waters below. I watched as he whirled around with the currents, going up and under, twisting and turning before disappearing around a bend downstream, sightless eyes reflected in the harsh glow of the afternoon sun.

I couldn't understand what had happened. At first I thought Rennsdale had somehow done it, but she still stood on the bridge, now watching me. Then I heard a rustling in the downed tree, and I looked just quickly enough to glimpse the hindquarters of something headed back through the leaves. It seemed to be about the size of a cocker spaniel. But even with the bobbed tail, it looked nothing like the back end of a dog.

Then I realized what it was. A bobcat. It had to be.

I stood and watched it dart up the side of a hill into the woods and just like that it was gone. I guess I stared after it for quite a while, trying to understand what had happened, until another big gust of wind came up and the bridge began another hula dance. Quickly, I reached the little tree and wrenched it off the end of the bridge and down the side of the hill into the raging brown waters of the creek, not far from where the maddened hog had hit.

Rennsdale was already settled in, licking a paw, when I climbed onto the Indian's saddle and opened the throttle, the planks rattling under our wheels like chattering teeth. Once I cleared the bridge I opened that bike up, and in a rooster tail of spraying mud, thundered up the slight hill and shot forward for home, Rennsdale flattening her little body against the groundsheet.

As I drove along in the setting sun, the

scene kept playing over and over in my mind. That hog, rushing at me with murder on its mind and, in deus ex machina fashion, another animal appearing out of nowhere to save my bacon — and then leaving before I could for sure know what it even was.

And then, my brain shifted into free-association, I guess, because I started thinking about what Pat had told me about the four old women, sitting at that table with a pentagram in front of them, plotting who knows what. As I examined that thought, Ma's voice from our conversation that morning came to me.

Our people, she had said, referring to Mrs. Davis and some others.

Our people. Her people. What did that mean?

Suddenly, I shivered, even though I'll bet it was still 90 degrees, because I once again heard the fervent conversation I'd had with David Jefferson in that St. Louis boarding house, when he'd told me about the cleansing and the clans and about how the Gabbers could actually change from human to hog, and do it to other people as well. He hadn't known whether the other clans — the cats and the snakes — could do the same thing.

Well, hell — maybe they could.

Suddenly, it all made sense — a weird nightmarish kind of sense, but one that was by damn true to itself, and true to all the feline encounters I'd had. The cat I caught reading my notes only a few days after I arrived in town. The cat at the cemetery that had led me to the

headstone over the mass grave. The cats that
always seemed to be following me when I set out
on foot. The cat that had talked to me a few
nights ago, there in the attic above the meeting. The more time I put between myself and
that night, the less sure I was that it had
actually spoken, but whatever had happened had
put me on my toes and kept me from what
could've been a damned deadly snake attack.

And then, there were those other, earlier,
conversations with Ma and Mrs. Davis, after I'd
tried to shoot the cat that had invaded my
room. It all came back around to what David had
told me about the clans and how the cats were
the ones that tried to keep the peace.

Was part of that job looking out for
Robert, the interloper? That's the only thing
I could figure. I was under some sort of
feline protection — especially, I figured,
after the four old ladies had their conclave
(I almost thought coven). That's why Mrs.
Davis had insisted on my taking a cat with me
wherever I went. Had the last snake attack,
the copperhead in the box that had angered Ma
so much, taken things to new heights? Were
those ladies — and their cats — protecting me
from Old Man Black and his serpents? And
maybe from the Gabbers, at least for right
now? And if they were, were they doing it
through cats — or, heaven help us, were they
cats?

Our people.

The chill skittered through me again.

Maybe they weren't only <u>people</u>. Maybe they were something more.

I looked over at Rennsdale, hunkered down in the sidecar. Now, John, the Indian was making its usual racket and the whipping wind added to the din around us. But somehow, in the midst of all that noise, I swear I heard that little cat purring.

Your pal and faithful correspondent,
Robert

ACKNOWLEDGMENTS

We extend our deepest thanks to Lara Bernhardt, Steven Wooley, Ray Riethmeier, and Bill Bernhardt for their time, insight, observations, and expertise.

ABOUT THE AUTHORS

Robert A. Brown has spent most of his working life in public education, serving as both a reading specialist and a principal, but he has also authored several nonfiction pieces dealing with the Great Depression and its popular culture, including western movies and the so-called "Spicy" magazines of the period. His work includes a piece on the legend of cowboy-movie star Tom Mix commissioned by the National Cowboy and Western Heritage Museum. An internationally known collector of nostalgic items such as movie paper, radio premiums, and pulp magazines, Brown supplied the art and wrote the text for Kitchen Sink Press's popular trading card series *Spicy: Naughty '30s Pulp Covers* and *Spicy: More Naughty '30s Pulp Covers*, which quickly became sold-out collector's items.

Brown initiated what became *The Cleansing*, writing letters on authentic period stationery to his old friend Wooley, using his deep knowledge of the 1930s to portray himself as the WPA employee beset by rural horrors who became *The Cleansing's* protagonist.

John Wooley made his first professional sale in the late 1960s, placing a script with the legendary *Eerie* magazine. He's now in his sixth decade as a professional writer, having written three horror novels with co-author Ron Wolfe, including *Death's Door*, which was one of the first books released under Dell's Abyss imprint and was also nominated for a Bram Stoker Award. His solo horror and fantasy novels include *Awash in the*

Blood, Ghost Band, and *Dark Within,* the latter a finalist for the Oklahoma Book Award.

Wooley is also the author of the critically acclaimed biographies *Wes Craven: A Man and His Nightmares* and *Right Down the Middle: The Ralph Terry Story.* He has co-written or contributed to several volumes of Michael H. Price's Forgotten Horrors series of movie books and co-hosts the podcast of the same name. His other writing credits include the 1990 TV film *Dan Turner, Hollywood Detective* and several documentaries, notably the Learning Channel's *Hauntings Across America.* Among the comics and graphic novels he's scripted are *Plan Nine from Outer Space,* the authorized version of the alternative-movie classic, as well as the recent collections *The Twilight Avenger* and *The Miracle Squad.*

Made in the USA
Columbia, SC
26 September 2020

21646755R00171